A LINGERING MELODY

Four years ago Carrie, naïve and innocent, had fallen in love with Matt Silver,
and they had lived a passionate and
tender dream—until one day he had left
her. Now he was back in her life, and
this time he had a power over her that
made her unable to refuse him anything
he asked . . .

A LINGERING MELODY

BY

PATRICIA WILSON

MILLS & BOON LIMITED
ETON HOUSE   18–24 PARADISE ROAD
RICHMOND   SURREY TW9 ISR

First published in Great Britain 1987
by Mills & Boon Limited

© Patricia Wilson 1987

Australian copyright 1987
Philippine copyright 1987
This edition

ISBN 0 263 75739 0

Set in Monotype Times 10.4 on 10.4 pt.
01-0787-58987

Typeset in Great Britain by
Associated Publishing Services
Printed and bound in Great Britain by
Collins, Glasgow

CHAPTER ONE

As THE big Qantas jet flew in low over London, Carrie felt a burst of panic. It was a long time since she had felt that and it was not in any way a physical fear; it was a great suffocating surge of anxiety, the frightening feeling that she wouldn't be able to cope, wouldn't be able to face familiar things again. Four years, and just the sight of England brought the pain back in a blinding rush as if there had been no time lapse, as if she was still young and heartbreakingly in love.

'Look! Mummy, look! London!' The excited voice, the little hand tugging at her sleeve as Gemma demanded her attention brought Carrie back to the present with a snap and Pippa's voice, almost identical but decidedly louder, joined in from the seat in front.

'The Queen lives here. Uncle Allan said so. Does she know we're coming?'

Carrie's cousin looked round from the seat in front to grin at her.

'Let's hope not! She has her own problems.'

Carrie laughed and leaned forward as Pippa continued to call from the seat beside Allan, demanding to know more about the city she had never seen before.

'Uncle Allan will tell you that. Speak more quietly, Pippa.'

'Oh, thank you, Caroline,' Allan grimaced good-naturedly before turning back. 'The only history I know I've made up myself, but I'll think of something.'

With Gemma content simply to stare down out of the plane and Pippa enthralled by Allan's astonishing tales of London, Carrie leaned back and closed her eyes, unwilling to feel the pain and the newly discovered panic, but powerless to prevent it.

Minutes to landing, and she would be back to where it had all started, back to where she had fought despair and almost lost the battle, and it would look just the same. Things didn't change much in four years, only people changed and now she had the twins, she was another person, and Matt—Matt was in America.

'Happy birthday, sweet sixteen.' The old song kept running round in her head, except that she had been nineteen and it seemed to have been a lifetime ago.

If he ever saw her again he wouldn't know her, wouldn't want to, but she would know him. She would know Matt anywhere, even in a crowd or blindfolded, she would know the deep quiet of his voice.

The touchdown jerked her back to reality and she realised with a feeling of shame that tears were stinging the back of her eyes. She needed the flurry of activity that landing brought to pull her out of it. Heavens, she hadn't even set foot on the ground yet and she was agonising over the dead past, thrown back so easily into a time she had struggled so hard to forget.

The twins were a real bundle of trouble and she was glad of that today. She and Allan had enough problems without Matt occupying her mind. Her eyes met Allan's as he stretched to his full six feet to reach for the cabin bags. He looked at her with a quick understanding, reassuring her as usual, winking broadly before scooping Pippa up into his arms, her little hands clinging tightly to his neck, threatening to choke him.

'Can you manage Gemma, Carrie?'

She nodded, smiling brightly, trying in her turn to reassure him. He had rescued her once, done everything for her, been her only friend and she had no intention of breaking up again. Allan needed all her help now and everything she could do would be little enough to repay him for his affection and steady support.

She picked up Gemma and made her way to the door, holding tightly to her daughter, following Allan and keeping her mind as calm as possible, reminding herself that she was not a girl any more. She had two children, had been Allan's personal assistant and run the Sydney office almost single-handed for nearly three years. Panic was not going to swamp her.

She was fair, her hair a mass of neatly cut curls the colour of ripe corn but the twins were flaxen-haired, the same clear, light gold as Allan's. It was odd when Matt was so dark but they had his eyes, the warm colour of honey. She tightened her lips and looked straight ahead, following her cousin and seeing Pippa's shining head rest against his shoulder. It was an amazing family likeness. Her mother and aunt had been fair too and so had Grandma Ellie when she was young.

'Viking ancestry!' Grandma Ellie had said proudly. 'They came well up into the Dales, you know!' Though how Grandma Ellie would have been able to cope with Vikings neither Carrie nor Allan had ever been able to imagine. According to her, rape and pillage were almost certain to take place anywhere from a line south of York or north of Hadrian's Wall. She had never once left the Dales in her whole life and it had taken both Carrie's pleading and Allan's stubborn insistence to convince her that nowadays Carrie would be perfectly safe in London. Well, they had both been wrong, but Grandma Ellie had never known.

Before they had left Sydney, Allan had booked them into a good hotel but it would probably be for the last time, they both knew that. Tomorrow, Allan would open up his flat and then they would have to take a good look at the future unless tonight's meeting secured some miraculous reprieve for Allan's business. Having run his affairs for so long, Carrie didn't expect that. His financial backers were demanding profits or blood and there were no profits yet. She was fully aware that tonight's meeting would be the beginning of the end for Croft Computers. They had been practically ordered back to England.

'Stop worrying like that,' Allan chided her as he hurriedly changed for the meeting and left Carrie to settle them into the hotel. But his cheerfulness did nothing to allay the alarm and depression that had been steadily growing for the last few days.

Taking stock of the situation, she realised that they had very little between them even if all their assets were pooled. Allan had a brilliant future—if he had one at all—and Carrie had a little money left that had come to her from Grandma Ellie. Then there were the twins to consider. It was a grim lip-biting future that she pondered as she got the girls ready for bed.

And it was so unexpected, so odd! Such a short time ago, their biggest backer Carter-Rousseau had seemed pleased, contented to let things run and wait for profits that were assured when suddenly a new and sinister picture had emerged. Carter-Rousseau's had completely changed and Carrie had begun to feel uncomfortably that Croft Computers was a struggling fish, hooked and being reeled in by a master angler, Allan's hard work ignored, his prospects discounted, only the kill a consideration.

She had realised that there had been a big stir in the City, new money poured into Carter-Rousseau and it had seemed like a good thing at the time. Obviously she had read it all wrong and she could only wait now for the result of this late-night meeting.

Allan was still not back when she put the twins to bed at seven. There were no protests. They were too tired to be any trouble and she was left with a minute to herself for the first time since Allan had gone to the meeting.

She looked at herself in the mirror as she left the children's room, still faintly astonished at what she saw. A face fined into maturity, the face of an efficient business assistant, the face of an accomplished mother. Yet inside she still felt the same, especially now in this city, so close to where Matt had entered her life and changed its course.

The barriers she had painstakingly built over the last four years against any thought of him fell in an agonising rush as she found her mind searching for him as she had wanted to search for him when he had left her. She felt once again as she had felt then, shy and bewildered in the bright lights of a big city.

Carrie had been excited and a little awestricken when she had been accepted at Redland Secretarial College. It had once been called Redland College for Young Ladies, in more genteel times, but now, lost in the heart of the city that had grown around it almost obliterating it, it stood, old and ivy-covered, on the edge of a quiet square, still with prestige but taking in a wider sweep of students.

There were many London businesses who scooped up their secretarial staff from Redland. Its practice of introducing budding private secretaries to the business world was as old as the college itself, an anachronism that should have gone out with the hansom cab and gaslight but which remained. It took the form of an alarming evening at one of the bigger hotels to show off young ladies and let them see the kind of wealthy, powerful people they would be expected to work with, a quick jab in the arm if efforts should be flagging after the first term. A star to hitch their wagon to.

And Carrie had felt lost in the enormous hotel, small and definitely scared like a field mouse in Piccadilly. The great chandeliers seemed to be showing up every bit of wear on her best blue dress. After a moment's relief when she realised that she would not be expected to sit at some long banqueting table, that there was a buffet, her consternation grew as it dawned on her that she would probably be expected to circulate—make bright conversation. As yet, she had made no real friends at College and her few acquaintances rapidly deserted her as she shrank even further into herself, making for the nearest wall and staying there —the survival instinct.

'This is your first time at this shindig?'

Carrie turned grateful eyes on the rather startling brunette who had come up to her and handed her a glass.

'Yes. Isn't it yours? Oh, I'm sorry. You're not at the College.' Belatedly, her eyes had taken in the cream silk dress and matching shoes, the professionally arranged hair. Not all the girls were hard up but they couldn't run to this sort of thing.

'I am at the College!' The girl laughed and took a second glass from a passing waiter. 'This is the third time I've done the course. I fail, deliberately! Being at College beats working any day and Daddy's paying—he couldn't care less. Besides, there's always a chance to get yourself a really well-off husband at these affairs if you play your cards carefully. Third time lucky. I hope!'

She raised her glass and drank deeply. Carrie hadn't touched hers except for a timid sip that had nearly choked her.

'I—don't like the look of many of them. I don't think I'd fancy working for them. They stare too much. I suppose they recognise that I'm fresh from the country and don't fit in very well.'

'I wasn't thinking of working for them,' the girl said a trifle sharply. 'And that's not why they're staring at you!'

At a loss for words, Carrie said nothing and after a while, the girl relented.

'What's your name?'

'Caroline Stuart. I'm from Yorkshire. The Dales.'

'You certainly look as if that might be true!' The sudden laugh took the sting out of her words. 'I'm Vivienne Trevere from London. Maybe I'll show you around when I'm not so busy.'

She winked at Carrie and prepared to move off, but stepped back straight away, her voice lowered to conspiracy.

'Now there's a catch! Unfortunately, he's immune to marriage, or so they say, in fact he's almost immune to the ladies altogether. At any rate, I got well and truly bounced,' she finished in surprise.

'Who?' Carrie's eyes followed the almost predatory gaze that Vivienne turned on the man who had just entered the room.

'Matthew Silver. Head of Silver Electronics. He's about thirty-two, a millionaire before he was twenty-eight, no attachments now, six feet two, luxury flat in London, country house not too far away, perfect were it not for his hang-up.' She reeled off his assets like a teleprinter.

'He told you all that? What's his hang-up?' Carrie couldn't take her eyes of him, and in her opinion he looked too cool and sardonic even to speak. His eyes were carelessly scanning the crowd, obviously looking for someone, and he found them—two lean-looking bespectacled men who had been talking animatedly to each other since she had arrived. They looked like bank managers—or spies, she couldn't decide which.

'His hang-up is a woman in America and no, he didn't tell me all that. I do my groundwork thoroughly, only in his case it was a waste of time. He told me two things, "hello" and "goodbye", and in between he stared over my head and nodded vaguely. I might have saved myself the trouble. He came close to shattering my confidence but I heard later that he had no trust in the female of the species after a heated

love affair. I should think that he's only called in to
see those two prawns. They're company lawyers,
salaried,' she added scathingly. 'One's from the
Matherson Ellis Corporation and the other one's from
Silver Electronics. I expect they're here to snoop and
listen in to conversations.'

She just drifted away, intent on her own affairs and
Carrie was intrigued by the serious conversation
between the two men and the newcomer, Matthew
Silver, though not a little disappointed that they were
not, after all, spies.

She was still staring at them when Matthew Silver
looked up, almost as if he sensed that someone was
watching him closely. He didn't even glance around,
his eyes found hers at once, compellingly direct,
holding her gaze over the heads of the chattering,
drinking crowd and she felt the colour rush to her
face as he watched her. It was almost as if her refused
to let her look away, and even so far away she knew
that he realised the effect he was having on her because
a slow half-smile tilted his mouth. It scared her because
he was not smiling at her. She tingled with sudden
shock, seeing his eyes narrow as his study of her
deepened in intensity, and she looked away quickly,
half turning so that she wouldn't accidentally look
again. For a second the most weird feeling had come
over her and her heart was racing with alarm. She
tried the drink again, carefully, managing not to
choke, although it still brought a little grimace of
distaste to her face.

Now she was even more trapped because she
couldn't even look round with any feeling of security.
She glanced up warily and a couple of the men seemed
as if they were about to come and speak to her. She
had no idea what to say if they did and she wondered
if she could simply sneak off unnoticed and head back
to her bedsit.

'It's no use trying to sink into the wall, the lights

are too bright and sooner or later, somebody's going to notice that you're not just a piece of panelling.' The deep amused voice had her spinning round to meet the equally amused eyes of the chairman of Silver Electronics.

'Oh! I'm not trying to do anything. I—I'm just standing here.'

'Hating every silly moment of it and feeling just a trifle over-exposed?' There was a sardonic edge to his voice that somehow disappointed her—and definitely scared her—and she looked at him as if she felt like begging him simply to go away.

'I've—I've never been to anything like this before. I'm afraid I can't just rush up to people and talk brightly. Maybe I'll get the courage to do it after a while.'

'God forbid!' She could see that his eyes were brown, a sort of warm dark honey colour with little lighter flecks of gold. They brought a warmth into the lean rather harsh darkness of his face. She had never spoken to a man like this before in her life—handsome, sure of himself, not a shining strand of his dark brown hair out of place.

'Do you know that you're staring?' His lips quirked with amusement on the question as he looked straight into the deep blue of her eyes, frightening her into taking a gulp of her drink. Before it had reached her lips, however, he had it from her, sliding it deftly on to the tray of a rather harrassed waiter.

'Bring me a lemonade with ice.' The waiter looked about to say that he had more than enough to do, before he saw who was speaking.

'Yes, Mr Silver. One second.' He disappeared smartly and Matthew Silver stuck a cheroot between his strong teeth, lighting it with a thin gold lighter. His watch was gold too, exquisite, expensive. Carrie was impressed by this subdued display of wealth, even his shirt must have cost . . .

'You're staring again.' He was looking at her across the flare of the lighter, the dancing flame making his cheekbones seem higher, his nose straighter and she blushed like a wild rose, tearing her eyes away.

'I'm sorry. I suppose it's because I'm a country bumpkin.'

'I see. I did wonder. Now that we have you safely classified, let's label you properly. What's your name?'

'Caroline. Caroline Stuart.'

'Good evening, Miss Stuart. I'm Matt Silver.'

'I know. Vivienne told me.'

'Who?' He was startled and them smiled wryly.

'Vivienne Trevere. I just met her and then you came in and . . . '

'What a fancy name. I'm afraid I don't know her but if it makes you feel that we've been properly introduced then I'm grateful to her.'

He was laughing at her, she knew, not openly but with a quiet relish that increased her embarrassment.

'It's—it's a really beautiful name—Vivienne.'

'And yours is what? Ordinary as befits a country wench?'

The waiter returned with the lemonade and Matt took it from the tray leaving a tip that looked large enough to buy a whole crateful and earned himself a look of surprised gratitude from the man.

'Your drink.' He handed it to her and leaned one broad shoulder against the wall, watching her.

'Thank you. I'm really thirsty. I didn't really like . . . ' He nodded, looking at her as if she were an interesting biological specimen.

'How old are you, Caroline Stuart?'

'I'm nineteen.' Her face flushed under the steady gaze of the honey-brown eyes as his eyebrows rose sceptically.

'Sixteen!' He corrected firmly, looking at her as if she were lying to achieve some dark and devious advantage.

'I'll be nineteen tomorrow!' His disbelief momentarily drowned her shyness and had her speaking sharply, to his obvious amusement.

'Ah! The big day. You'll be going home to celebrate?'

'No.' She felt a little burst of self-pity. 'It's too far and I can't really afford it anyway. Besides, it's Friday and I've got lectures all day. It's the first time that . . . '

'Where is home?' He was still watching her interestedly, his eyes narrow against the smoke.

'Yorkshire. The Dales.' She wasn't going to be drawn into talking about herself because he wouldn't be interested, in fact she couldn't reckon up why he was here at all. His whole attitude seemed to be a subtle rebuke as if she had come here by herself for similar reasons to Vivienne.

'So, that's where you got the colouring. Hair like ripe corn, violet eyes.'

'They're blue.' He was embarrassing her and she wanted to tell him that now he was the one who was staring, but she dared not, he was far too overpowering to be snubbed by anyone. She wished he would go.

'Violet!' he insisted. 'Like the shy flowers that hide in the woods. Explain the hair.' Suddenly he was smiling, not laughing at her, not reproaching her subtly any more, and she felt less inclined to take to her heels.

'Grandma Ellie says we have Viking ancestors.' She said it with a little laugh and he stared at her so hard that her new-found confidence fled as quickly as it had come.

'What do you imagine that Grandma Ellie would think of this affair?' His hand took in the room, his eyes never leaving hers. 'What, for example, would she make of me?'

'She'd think that—that you were rather splendid.'

She looked into her lemonade and he gave a quick hard laugh before straightening up, seeming suddenly to tire of this conversation that Carrie, after all, had never introduced.

'I think that's probably your own bewildered opinion,' he observed dryly. 'I would imagine that Grandma Ellie would have an entirely different one, one that I wouldn't much care for but which I would be forced to agree with. This is not the place for babies, Caroline Stuart.'

His eyes were no longer warm as they swept the room, resting deliberately on a couple of the men who had been watching her, men who now looked carefully away. 'It's time you were home and safely tucked up in your bed.'

'I'm capable of taking care of myself!' she said quietly, her face flushing as she finally got the drift of his remarks and understanding of Vivienne's tart comment dawned on her. 'I'm nineteen!'

His eyes narrowed at the little sign of her distress but his face did not soften.

'Not until tomorrow. For tonight, watch your step and keep Grandma Ellie firmly in mind.'

'Hello, Caroline. I lost you for a minute. ' Vivienne Trevere came up, her eyes flashing signals at Matt Silver which he ignored completely, but her appearance seemed to make up his mind and he collared the waiter again.

'Call a taxi for Miss Stuart, will you? She's not well. This should take care of it.' The man's fingers closed over a note and he looked sympathetically at Carrie.

'I'll have one outside for you in two shakes, Miss.'

'She looks all right to me!' Her efforts obviously pointless, Vivienne glared at Carrie.

'She's barely hanging on. ' He didn't so much as glance at Vivienne. Instead he looked sternly at Carrie. 'Use the taxi. Go straight home. Be thankful you've got a grandma.'

She didn't really know what he meant but she was grateful to him because now she could escape. When the waiter signalled her from the door, she turned to Matt Silver but he was already moving away.

'Thank you.' He merely nodded disinterestedly, already returning to his intense companions, his mind on something else. The only sign that he had heard her thanks was a brief gesture of farewell from the hand that held the cheroot, and Carrie supposed that she was his good deed for the day. Anyway, she would never see him again. He certainly wouldn't want a secretary who hid by walls and had to have a lemonade. But she was grateful, more than he would ever know. He had given her an excuse in case she was questioned next day although she couldn't think of anyone, even those on the college staff, who would have the temerity to question Matt Silver.

Next day, she was questioned very closely though by Vivienne Trevere and several other girls. What had he said? Was he interested? It was all a little sickening, a little shocking, and so was their obvious disbelief at her replies. Apparently he had left almost immediately and the coincidence was too much for them to swallow.

The grilling they gave her had the unfortunate effect of bringing him to the forefront of her mind. A good night's sleep, the rush to be on time, and her first few lectures had dulled some of the drama of the night before—and it had been dramatic for someone who had spent much of her life in a cottage on a windswept hill, four miles from the nearest market town. Being rescued by a cool, handsome, wealthy man had made an impression on her that she had been at pains to shrug off. Now it all came back. The frightening feeling that had been akin to recognition when their eyes had met across the room, the deep, amused sound of his voice and his air of calm authority.

Several times she had to pull herself back into the present and she was glad when at four-thirty her last lecture ended and she could escape through the big main doors and out into the relative peace of the old square. If she hurried, she could get the tube before the main rush-hour passengers. Carrie slung her bag over her shoulder, clutching her books and walking briskly across the road.

He was there. She had been too deep in thought to see him before but he was leaning against the bonnet of a long, low car, a bright red car that looked too expensive to be taken out on the road. For a second she hesitated, wanting to back stealthily away. He wouldn't want to talk to her and hear her repeated thanks, but he was looking at her and she couldn't simply turn on her heel and walk off. Whoever he was waiting for, she had at least to acknowledge him.

He watched her come hesitatingly forward and then slowly drew himself up to his full height.

'Good afternoon, Caroline Stuart.'

He was looking down at her with a half-smile on his face and she didn't know what to say except, 'Hello, Mr Silver.'

'Polite child.' He reached into the car and pulled out a huge bouquet of white roses. 'Happy birthday, sweet sixteen.'

'They're for me?' She looked at him wide-eyed, unsure whether or not to take them, very wary.

'They are.' He put them in her arms, his smile widening. 'It's the right colour, isn't it? White for York and red for Lancaster? I wouldn't want to start any trouble.'

'Yes, they're lovely. Thank you.' She was still stunned, shaking a little. 'Why did you . . . ? I mean . . . ' It sounded terribly ungrateful but he didn't seem to mind.

'It seemed such a shame. All alone for the first time ever on your birthday.'

He had noticed her little burst of self-pity, then, and followed her chain of thought. It made her feel guilty, as if she were imposing on him, and she buried her face in the flowers.

'You can put them on the table when you have your birthday party. You are having a party?'

'No.' It was out before she thought. 'I told you, it's too far to go home and Jenny's going away for the weekend. She's my flatmate.' He just looked at her, smiling, and she added in a flurry, 'She's got a boyfriend, you see—in Wolverhampton . . . ' Her voice trailed away and he nodded, his face perfectly serious.

'I'll slot that piece of information away for future reference. It's nice to know about somebody in Wolverhampton.'

He was laughing even though his face was perfectly serious and she felt gauche, pretty close to the sixteen that he had called her and she wanted badly to escape.

'It's a lovely car,' she said quickly, looking at it to avoid looking at him.

'A Ferrari GTO.'

'Does it go very fast?'

'You're thinking of stealing it?' He was laughing openly now and her cheeks flushed until she felt as red as the car.

'Thank you for the flowers, Mr Silver and for the taxi last night. Goodbye.' She started to walk past him but his hand on her arm and his quiet voice stopped her.

'I'm sorry.'

She raised quietly accusing eyes. 'Being nineteen doesn't necessarily make me a moron, Mr Silver.'

'I never imagined that it did. Put my rudeness down to an unexpected attack of nerves and forgive me?'

When she didn't answer, his hand fell away from her arm but his eyes were warm and smiling as she met his gaze.

'I wanted to offer to take you out to a birthday dinner, but it occurred to me that you just might start to run, or send for Grandma Ellie to tackle me. She wouldn't approve of me, would she?' he added softly.

'No.' His apparent uncharacteristic diffidence made her smile as her own embarrassment lessened. 'She thinks that London is a dangerous place.' Her eyes twinkled. 'She says it's full of . . . '

'Fast cars and loose women?' He finished for her, his smile widening into an attractive grin. 'Has she ever been here?'

'No.' Carrie was laughing now. 'She's never been out of the Dales, but she has fund of strict advice and iron-strong rules.'

He nodded, his eyes warm and amused.

'Well, it's a fast car, but I can't see any women about who would obviously fit the required category, only a mere babe with violet eyes.'

And she suddenly felt the need to cast aside caution, to defy Grandma Ellie and her rules quietly, to stay longer in the company of this tall, powerful man with warm eyes who made her tingle inside.

'If you mean it, I'd like to come.'

She sounded a bit breathless and he looked at her intently.

'You're quite sure, Caroline Stuart? You're not just saying that to get yourself out of the tricky situation that I've landed you in?'

'You haven't.' Carrie tried to be as calm as possible, tilting her chin proudly. 'I can easily walk off and leave you standing here. I can return the flowers and just—just go.'

'But you decided to take the big risk of a lifetime?' He looked at her for a second longer and then opened the car door. 'Hop in then. I'll take you back to your flat and then I'll know where to collect you.' He looked at her reassuringly when she hesitated. 'I don't eat little girls,' he said softly. 'You're perfectly safe.'

She felt perfectly foolish so she got in, and, anyway,

her legs were shaking and it was good to sit down in the warm luxury of the car.

'Where exactly?' He had been frowning ever since she had told him where she lived and now as they came to streets she recognised she was able to direct him herself. He looked as if he might be thinking that somebody would steal his car wheels.

'Up here. It's perfectly respectable.'

'For whom?' He turned into her street and she had to admit to herself that it looked a pretty wretched place. In fact, she had been very miserable here until she had got used to it.

'Where's your flat?' He was now looking thoroughly ferocious.

'Third house. It's a bedsit, really. They all are on this side. I share mine with . . . '

'I know! Jenny!' He stopped at the door and looked up at it in disgust. 'Listen! By seven o'clock it's going to be dark. Don't you dare take one step outside this door until I call for you!'

'All right but . . . '

'But nothing! I hope you heard me clearly, young lady? I don't normally have to say the same thing twice!'

'I'll wait. Thanks for the lift, Mr Silver.'

'The name is Matt!' he rasped, giving her the same ferocious look he had given the house. 'Seven o'clock —sharp!'

She hadn't the faintest idea what to wear, and now that he had gone she felt just a little scared at the way she had accepted. She didn't know him, after all, and anyway, he would probably think that she was too forward, like Vivienne.

Having tortured herself for ages with ridiculous worries, Carrie found that she had to rush. She washed and dried her hair, dismayed to find that the short crisp curls were unmanageable, more tightly curled than ever. She couldn't wear the blue dress, she'd worn that last night, so she put on a white dress that she hardly ever wore because it made her look too young. Looking at herself in the mirror, she shrugged resignedly. Nothing would make her look sophisticated, she was herself and that was all she could do.

But when he arrived and she went downstairs and stepped into the street, she cringed at the look in his eyes.

'Point taken, sweet sixteen,' he remarked drily, his eyes on her crisp curls, her bewildered eyes and the dress that hugged her slim waist and flared around her slender legs. 'Although there was no need whatever to make the point.'

'I don't understand.' She'd managed to annoy him and he suddenly smiled, taking her arm and helping her into the car.

'I don't suppose you do, at that,' he remarked softly.

Too shy and unsure to make conversation, she surreptitiously watched his long capable hands on the wheel as he wove in and out of the traffic. Everything was new and exciting, a little frightening, and she still didn't know if she had done the right thing by agreeing to go out with him. She kept her mind firmly away from home and the utter shock that would have been on her grandmother's face if she could see Carrie now. She supposed that Allan would have been shocked too and not a little annoyed but there was a thrill in being with Matt Silver even though he did treat her as if he were a substitute father.

It was at a really quiet place by the river that he eventually stopped, and although it was full there were none of the brilliant lights to alarm her. She was greatly relieved, until it occurred to her that he wouldn't want to be seen with her in any brightly lit place anyhow. Yesterday he had rescued her and today he had come because he was sorry to think that she was lonely on her birthday. Clearly, in spite of the alarming air of power about him, he was kind and considerate, but naturally he wouldn't want to be seen dragging someone that he referred to as a babe into any smart place of his normal evenings out.

Although he seemed to be well enough known here—at least, he stood talking to the head waiter for several minutes before leading her to the table. She couldn't hear the conversation but from time to time the man glanced in her direction and when he finally nodded and walked away, he was grinning all over his face. It did nothing for her confidence and Matt sighed loudly as he settled her in her chair and seated himself opposite.

'All right! Let's clear the air before we begin to eat, Caroline Stuart.' He looked steadily at her giving her a funny little shiver inside. 'I brought you here, not because I'm alarmed at being seen with you in what you clearly imagine are 'my usual haunts', but because you didn't seem to me to be too happy last night in the glitter of a big hotel. Now, will you stop thinking self-destructively and take a more positive look at life?'

'I didn't think . . . '

'Oh, but you did!' he interrupted firmly. 'Every thought that passes through your head flashes up on that face in large clearly visible letters.'

'I'm not very sophisticated, am I?' She looked up and as quickly looked away. 'You're right about the bright lights, though. Thank you.'

'Well, we progress,' he murmured softly. 'At least you didn't say "Thank you, Mr Silver". As to sophistication, no, you've none of that. You're not a raving beauty either—not yet. Girls like you, girls with fresh skins and clear eyes, girls with heads covered with golden curls, are not made for sophistication, so don't try it. Apart from the nasty shock it would give Grandma, you'd look fairly ridiculous.'

Any little dregs of confidence that she had left her

then very abruptly and she sat in silence until he reached across and covered her hand with his.

'Fatherly advice is never appreciated at the time,' he observed, smiling into her eyes when she looked up, and she had to admit to herself that his attitude since she had met him had been little short of fatherly. It was a bit of a disappointment on her first major outing but at least it made her feel safe.

'The food's slow to arrive here, but definitely worth waiting for like all good things. Would you like to dance while we wait?' He nodded to the crowded dance floor where people were circling slowly to the music of a three-piece band. At her obvious pleasure he led her out on to the dance floor before she had time to worry about what it would be like when he held her. It was like dancing with a rather nice uncle and she relaxed at once, her skill pleasing and surprising him.

'Ah! You've danced a lot, Miss Stuart,' he teased gently and she nodded, laughing up into his face.

'Allan and I used to dance every week.'

'Your boyfriend?' He looked down at her but she laughed and shook her head.

'My cousin. More like a brother, really. Grandma brought us both up together when our parents were killed.'

'When was that?' His hands suddenly felt warmer and, in an odd way, comforting although she didn't need any comfort now.

'Oh, a long time ago. I don't often think about it now. I was nine and Allan was fifteen. My mother and Allan's were sisters. They were going to York, my parents and his, when a lorry . . . '

'I'm sorry. That's what happens when you dig into other people's lives, you irritate old wounds. Look, the meal's arrived.'

He was careful not to ask her anything else but she found herself telling him about the happiness of life in the isolated cottage, about the farm close by where Allan used to live, and he seemed interested.

'Is he a farmer now?'

'No, an engineer.' She kept well away from the mention of computers and the small firm that Allan had just succeeded in launching. Silver Electronics was a little too close to Allan's own field, and she didn't want him to think that she was interested in him for anything like that.

Interested in him! She suddenly blushed hotly and stopped talking. She hoped that this thought hadn't flashed up on her face. He had called his advice fatherly and that was exactly what he was being. She remembered Vivienne Trevere's words and realised that the only reason she was here tonight was that he didn't consider her to be a woman at all. She was merely a little girl being given a birthday treat. She was not receiving any of the cynicism that he apparently reserved for women.

She was saved from any chance of his reading her expression, however, as all the lights suddenly dimmed and the head waiter came into the room bearing a cake, its candles alight, and placed it in front of her as everyone began to clap.

'Don't forget to wish,' Matt said softly as she stared at it in astonished gratitude, her laughter struggling with tears. Her eyes were almost too blurred to read the writing in pink icing on the white cake, 'Happy Birthday Sweet Sixteen'. She looked up into his smiling face and the laughter won: she felt no embarrassment whatever, even when the little band struck up with 'Happy Birthday'.

'I've had a lovely evening,' she said quietly on the way back. He only nodded, as distant and preoccupied since the meal as if he had already taken her home. No doubt he thought again that it was way past her bedtime.

'The meal was lovely,' she ventured timidly, and his

eyes were suddenly laughing as he looked across at her, a quick, slanting look that made her heart jump.

'You expected chips and beans with a glass of milk to follow?' She couldn't think of any reply. He was altogether too much for her.

At her door, he took her hand and looked at her for a long time, his face serious, and then he simply said that he wouldn't drive away until she was safely inside.

It was only when Carrie was back in her room, the sound of the car fading further away, that she realised what his last words had been: 'Goodbye.' Of course, she had expected nothing else. He had been driven to this kindly act because of her bewilderment at the brilliantly lit hotel, and maybe he had also realised her loneliness. If he was still in love with someone who had let him down, then he was probably lonely himself and recognised her need.

It had not gone unnoticed that Matt had met her with flowers from college and that she had driven away with him. Vivienne Trevere was deeply interested and also, apparently, annoyed.

'Don't expect it to continue,' she had warned drily. 'Once bitten, twice shy, and he's not the sort of man to be bitten a second time. I did tell you that he's had an unhappy love affair. He's utterly cynical about the female of the species now. Nobody even gets to first base with Matthew Silver any more. He's probably still pining after his lost lady love, some American beauty called Yvette Something-or-other. Don't start getting all moonstruck about him.'

'I wasn't getting anything about him,' Carrie had managed to get out, her shyness disappearing in a fit of unusual anger. 'He took me to dinner because I was lonely on my birthday, nothing more! I don't expect to see him again. He's just a very nice man. He was fatherly, even!'

'You must be even younger than you look!' Vivienne

had laughed in surprise. 'Men come in one shape only—wolf shape. I suppose his basic instincts are still intact, although after an American film star, I must admit he's got me puzzled, picking on you. Still, maybe it's because you're an exact opposite, not much of a threat. Watch your step though, child.'

Carrie knew that she wouldn't have to watch anything though. Matthew Silver had said goodbye clearly and finally, and she was glad that he had bounced Vivienne when she had pursued him. If he had been hurt once then he could do well to keep clear of someone like Vivienne. She didn't like to think of him being hurt again. Oddly enough, he looked too strong ever to be hurt so he must have been deeply in love. She wondered how long ago it had been and if he would ever recover. Still, it was none of her business. She would never see him again.

CHAPTER TWO

THE sound of Allan's key in the main door of the suite snapped Carrie smartly back to the present and the look on his face, before he had had time to alter his expression, told her most of what she had been waiting to hear.

'No panic. It's not over yet.' He slumped tiredly into a chair, loosening his tie. 'They can't seem to make up their minds. They're torn between avarice and caution because they know that in a couple of years Croft Computers will be going a bomb. My new equipment opens up endless possibilities in Australia, Africa and South America and they'd like the chance of high profits. I think it would have been all right, except for one man there. They all seemed to be mesmerised by him and he was totally icy, just about the most unsympathetic man I've ever seen! He's one of the new members of the board. Remember that you told me that new people and money had come into Carter-Rousseau? Well, I wish they hadn't! The old fuddy-duddies who worried me so much when I first approached them now looked like kindly old relatives. This new chap's a different proposition, hunter-killer class, if he was a submarine!' He smiled wryly, looking already defeated in spite of his initial cheerful greeting and Carrie felt a burst of anger at the way he was being treated.

'Are the whole board going to let one man dictate to them? What did he say to convince them, or are they just scared of him?'

'Good money after bad was the general theme of

his warning, but he didn't really need to say anything to have them worried. If he had just sat silently until they had all said yes and he had then quietly said "No", they would all have agreed. He's got them scared just by being himself and they mostly deferred to him. Why he didn't simply tell me the worst and put me out of my misery, God knows! Anyway, there's a big dinner tomorrow night and I've been—invited. At least that was the word used, though the way Silver said it was more like an order to my own execution!'

'Silver!' For one frightening moment Carrie's heart seemed actually to stop beating. 'Is that the name of the new man?'

'That's him,' Allan sighed in disgusted weariness. 'Matthew Silver, Silver Electronics. God! I could have done with him on my side! He's a giant in the electronics business. He must know that Croft Computers is a winner. I can't understand his aggression, not with his knowledge!'

Carrie could, though. The feeling of being reeled in had been sheer instinct, and although everything inside her said that it was an impossibility, she knew in her heart that it was not. Cold fear raced over her skin as she stared at Allan, unable to think of a thing to say. He knew nothing about her time with Matt, had no idea who was the father of her children and even if there was now just a small chance that Allan's firm would survive, if he ever found out about Matt then the firm would be finished because he would cast aside his own future in his rage at the way Matt had treated her. She was ensnared by her own past, struggling in the bottom of the net, afraid to say anything at all.

'Will you come with me, Carrie?' Allan was saying, clearly not noticing her suddenly pale face. 'Apparently there'll be plenty of ladies there and you have all the details of the firm's finances at your fingertips. I don't know how they're going to play it, but I expect that at these dos businesses are made and broken by a few quiet words while they eat. Silver asked if you could come.'

'Me!' Carrie couldn't prevent the little gasp of fear and surprise. Not that she was really surprised, she told herself; she knew who Matt was trawling for, the only question was, why?

'Yes, well, not you specifically. He wants to hear from the person who knows the accounts of the firm inside out, no paper work, he told me coldly, apparently a quiet chat will do. You can drag me out when I faint,' he added with a cheerfulness that he was clearly not feeling.

'Count me in,' she said quietly, her mind suddenly racing as she tried to organise her thoughts and quiet her fears. She had never, except for the first brief meeting, feared Matt, although she had always known that he was a person greatly to be feared. But he had been her whole life for a short time, a wonderful time, he had been loving, protective, perfect. The thought that there would ever come a day when she would want to run and hide merely at the sound of his name would have seemed laughable then. 'We'll have to stay here for another day, then,' she told Allan, with the determination she had developed over the last few years. 'A good hotel can easily produce a reputable babysitter. I'll fix it up in the morning and then I'll nip out and get something extravagant to wear. I've still got a bit of money left. We'll call it an investment.'

'You'll really rock them,' Allan laughed, both amused and grateful for her support. 'I can see it now! What the beautiful cousin of the latest bankrupt wore!'

As usual, they parted in laughter, but the smile died from Carrie's face when she was securely in her own room, hidden from Allan's keen eyes. She had not thought that Matt would ever find her or that he would even try. Why should he? He, after all, had been the one to leave, the one with a past that called him back. She could think of no crime that she had committed, except loving him too much to be willing to be just another girl.

Even so, it was too much of a coincidence. He knew that Allan Croft was her cousin and although he had never known about Allan's contract in Australia it would have been relatively simple for somebody with Matt's wealth and connections to trace him. His vindictiveness could only be because of her, and Carrie paced the room in an agony of worry, wondering what else he knew and feeling as lost and vulnerable as she had when he had left her to go to America over four years ago.

She found the right dress within half an hour of beginning her search the next day—layer upon layer of lemon chiffon, utterly frothy and extravagant, the lightly boned bodice edged with gold. It left her tanned shoulders bare and she knew it would look stunning with the heavy antique gold necklace and bracelet that Grandma Ellie had hoarded and then left to her.

Even though she was tanned, even though she had suffered and matured, her short crisp curls and her wide violet eyes still made her wary of trying for any sophisticated look. She was herself and the dress made the best of it. She looked nineteen again. Only the price was wrong but she gulped down the shock and paid up courageously, but a look in the mirror that evening convinced her that every penny had been well spent. She was armed for the battle.

'Not so grim, love, not so grim,' Allan cautioned with a chuckle as their taxi dropped them at a Park Lane Hotel. 'Don't spoil the fairytale look by showing that you're really the witch. Let's keep that information strictly in the family.'

As usual, his humour relaxed her and she almost floated in on his arm, her face radiant, not even unnerved when she found all eyes on them. Of course they had been waiting for Allan like so many vultures gathered to dine and she could not have expected that their entrance would go unnoticed. There was no obvious sign that Matt had arrived and she felt that if he had already been there, she would have known. At least she would be able to get used to being in the glitter of this place with these people before he struck at her in whatever way he had planned. She did not expect to get away this evening without having to face him.

'You look quite beautiful. They'll simply forget that I'm here.' Allan's whisper gave her some hope that her presence might help, in some small way. If the news was bad, as Carrie expected it to be, then at least he could stalk out, his lady on his arm like the hero in an epic film. She and Allan would not slink away in defeat, even if they felt like it. Her chin rose and she sharpened her wits.

She needed them. In the ante-room they were offered cocktails and she found herself surrounded by strangers as Allan was reluctantly dragged from her side. People she had never seen before in her life offered her endless opportunities to refill her glass, which she refused, and plied her with endless questions about the great outback, which she had been far too busy ever to visit.

Although still feeling as though she stood on the deck of a small but honourable fighting ship while the enemy fleet closed in for the kill, Carrie coped with the situation quite easily. There was so much wealth gathered here, so much luxury, and Allan had spent endless months in the heat and dust in Australia, working like a demented slave, flying out to modify his equipment as new and different ores came from the ground. These people, who thought it was all some great adventure, were about to ruin him, to cancel out all that hard work, all the sweat and bone-aching tiredness, and she forgot all about Matt in her dislike of them, her eyes flashing with barely concealed annoyance at the questions.

In the midst of listening to an animated discussion of totally baseless opinions on Australia, Carrie looked up and her courage deserted her in one great leap of the heart. She had been glittering with a mixture of pride and annoyance, but now she was defenceless and beaten by one look from Matthew Silver.

He stood on the edge of the circle of noise that surrounded her, and she had no idea how long he had been watching her. For a moment her mind winged back to their first meeting as his eyes held hers in a keen and punishing stare that had her legs trembling immediately. Unable to help herself, she searched his face, her violet eyes wide and fascinated as she looked for some sign of the man who had taken her into his life and then carelessly let her slip from it. But he was not there.

The honey-coloured eyes were cold and sardonic, the harshly perfect face without emotion, and Allan's words came back to her with terrifying clarity. Hunter-killer. He had trapped her, reeled her in from thousands of miles away, and why, she had no idea.

She looked round frantically for Allan, no longer the one to support him, needing his help desperately, but there was no sign of him. When she turned back, Matt was in front of her, close enough to touch her, close enough for her to smell the faint, tangy, masculine smell that was her sensual memory of him. His dinner jacket was smoothly tailored, his hair shining perfection, and there the resemblance to the man she had loved ended.

'Do you think that I could have a word with Mrs Haley, gentlemen?' His eyes were on Carrie as he spoke, glittering now with an unholy humour that she had never seen in him before, his lips tilted in a smile with no warmth. His tone left them with little alternative and they drifted away as if they had received an order, leaving Carrie to face a man who looked at her with ill-concealed menace.

'You haven't changed a bit,' he said softly and coldly, his eyes skimming over her with dislike. 'Still so beguiling, so innocent, so defenceless.'

'You haven't changed either.' How could she still feel anything for him when he had treated her so cruelly? He had almost destroyed her, but even now, with the once-warm eyes coldly on her, his face hard and still, she had to steel herself not to whisper his name.

'Oh, but I have changed, Mrs Haley,' he corrected harshly. 'I'm older, harder, wealthier and filled with malevolence. One keeps up a reasonably benevolent face in public but the thirst for revenge is always there, a mere whisper below the surface.'

Twice he had called her Mrs Haley, his eyes not missing the plain golden band on her finger, the ring she and Allan had bought when they invented a father for the twins. She had put it on by herself and wept by herself, longing to be back in the security of Matt's arms, to be wearing his ring.

Her embarrassment at being an unmarried mother had led to the wearing of the ring and to a story that she had told so often that it almost seemed true, that Kevin Haley was real and not just a figment of her imagination.

'I see you found someone else to dress you in the manner to which you became accustomed,' he continued savagely before she could ask how he knew her name. 'I always wondered why you didn't take all the things I bought you when you left me. No doubt you thought you'd found a better prospect, someone perhaps closer to your radiant age. Well, I don't know about Haley's prospects but if your future is in any way reliant on your cousin then I can tell you that after tonight, his prospects are nil. If Croft Computers financed that dress then you'd better make it last a long, long time.'

'No decision has been taken yet,' she whispered, her

eyes on his cold face, her heart aching at his savage voice.

'The decision was taken the moment I found out where you were,' he grated with cruel satisfaction. 'All I had to do then was wait until I could buy into Carter-Rousseau and become a major shareholder. I'm also here as the visiting expert. The board may be gathered in force—after all, this dinner was planned weeks ago—but to them Croft Computers is only a minor pen stroke on the agenda. To me, it's the reason for my day. The decision is mine. I've made it!'

'You'll ruin a firm with wonderful prospects because of me?' Carrie's wide-eyed accusation left him stony-faced.

'Because of you,' he agreed with bitter satisfaction. 'Believe me, Mrs Haley, I've mellowed over the last four years. At first, my only desire was to kill you!'

Carrie stood stunned by the vindictiveness of his tone, by the hard reality that she was the one who had ruined Allan when he had done everything for her. But Matt had left her! Gone to another woman, gone back to her when she had called him!

Anger rose above all other feelings and as Allan finally made it back to her side she slipped her arm through his and nodded a cool farewell to Matt, speaking with a vindictiveness of her own.

'Darling, I've been looking all over for you! Thank goodness you're back. I'm bored to tears. Do you think we could go into the dining-room now?'

Matt stared after them as they left, his face as cold as stone and she felt hatred burning into her back.

'I take it from your face and from the face of our friend that it's no go?' Allan said glumly as they walked away. 'Did he want to know about the business?'

'Not a thing,' she said with as much calm as she could muster. 'He's not a man to plead with, and as to wanting to know things, it seems he's already made up his mind. I think this dinner is perhaps just a way to send Croft Computers out with a bang.'

'A whimper would have done,' Allan confided sourly. 'Still, I can see that a man like that would want to dig the knife in as far as possible.'

If only he knew! Carrie clung to Allan's arm, needing his support, her conscience tearing her apart. Without her he would have been a success. Matt would never have interested himself in Carter-Rousseau and even if he had, he would have seen the prospects that stretched like a rainbow in front of Allan's firm. All she could do was agonise to herself. She dared not tell Allan.

All through the meal, Carrie felt Matt's eyes on her, burning into her with so much hatred that she could have wept in front of everyone for the love she had once thought they shared. Only her loyalty to Allan and her pride stopped her from jumping up and running out into the darkness.

Matt had by no means finished with her, though. The moment the meal was over and the ordered affair became a mere milling around of people again, as the movement of millions of pounds became a matter for almost nonchalant discussion, he collared her again.

'So, where is Mr Haley then? Minding the babies while you wine and dine with Cousin Allan?' he enquired sarcastically.

She stiffened in fright, terrified about what he knew, her face paling at this seemingly total grip he had on her affairs.

'You—know about the twins?'

'I know about the twins!' he agreed with asperity. 'I know about every item in your life. Only the elusive Mr Haley has ducked from my grasp. He doesn't really concern me though. I merely ask out of polite interest. Where's Prince Charming hiding?'

She suddenly wanted to blurt out the truth about Gemma and Pippa, to wipe that look from his face, to see him stunned and demolished, but she held her tongue. He was rich, powerful and heartless. The knowledge that the twins were his would put a weapon into his hands that he would not hesitate to use. The name of Kevin Haley had kept her safe for a long time and she had spoken of him with enough conviction to satisfy everyone for four years. Matt was no different from anyone else.

'Kevin, my husband, disappeared,' she said quietly, almost choking on the oft-repeated lie.

'Disappeared?' The sardonic voice, none of the deep, rich warmth left, made her temper flare. 'Left you, went up in a puff of smoke or became invisible?'

'He disappeared at sea, in Australia where we lived. And no, he didn't leave me, Mr Silver. Contrary to your obvious beliefs people don't normally walk out on me. One example of that was all I needed. You hold the record!'

'Oh? I left you, did I?' he bit out savagely. 'And it didn't take you long to get fixed up with Mr Haley, did it? How old are those twins?'

Oddly enough, her instincts had been preparing her for this ever since she had realised that Matt was back in the picture. If she told him the truth he would know at once what had happened and his amused satisfaction would kill her. He would have another weapon.

'Three and a half exactly!' She looked straight at him and his face darkened in a flare of rage.

'Two months after I left Florida! Straight from my bed into another! And I thought you were all starry-eyed and innocent! You little . . . '

'I was innocent enough when I met you,' she interrupted coldly, her anger keeping her on her feet when she wanted to sink to the floor. 'And I do not wish to continue this conversation, Mr Silver, nor do I have to. I'm not nineteen any more. I no longer stand by walls with my thumb in my mouth, waiting to be rescued by bright executives.'

'No!' he ground out. 'You're a big girl now! You're certainly no longer starry-eyed!'

'You dealt with that very competently,' Carrie said quietly. 'There are no stars left for me to see. Now, if you wish to discuss the firm's finances, then that presumably is why I am here and I would like to get on with it.'

For a second he stared at her, his own face suddenly pale, looking for one brief moment lost for words. Then he shook his head, his face hard as ever.

'You are not here to discuss anything, Mrs Haley,' he said bitingly. 'You're here because I wanted to see how you looked after all these years. I wanted you to be quite sure who was wielding the axe and I wanted you to have no doubts as to why. Well, I've seen you. You look just the same on the outside and as to the inside, you're probably the same there too. I was just too ensnared to notice for four years. One has to step back and take a good look. Thank you for the look. Goodbye!'

He simply walked off leaving her standing, shattered and lost, his brief signal of farewell reminding her of another time, so long ago, when he had walked off and left her standing. Then, he had been sending her home in a taxi, making sure that she was safe. Now he was intent on destroying everything she touched. She tried to find comfort in the fact that his biggest weapon was still hidden from him: he had two beautiful children but he would never know. The thought only brought a wave of deep misery and she was still standing lost and forlorn when Allan found her.

'Any further developments on the war front?' he asked wryly. 'Nobody is saying a thing to me except to enquire about the great barren wastelands, which they seem to imagine cover the entire area of Australia.'

'I think you were right,' she said quietly. 'The

decision is with Silver, and he's made of stone. We may as well go home.'

She was quite right. No decision was announced to Allan and as far as he was concerned, the whole ordeal had been a complete waste of time. But Carrie knew differently. Her debt to Allan was now greater that it had ever been before. If she had not been with Allan in Australia, if she had simply stayed out of his life, then Matt would never have interested himself in Allan's affairs. Because of her and her alone, he would ruin Allan.

Apparently he had shrugged off the fact that he had been the one to leave. Perhaps he had even intended to come back, certainly he had never seemed to want her to be out of his sight. But what was she supposed to have done about the fact that there was another woman? If she had never found the photograph, the letter, would things have been different? If she had been older, wiser, less in love, would she have waited and faced him with her knowledge? It was too late now and in any case, Matt had turned into stone.

Now she was the villain, the scarlet woman who went from one man to another. What would his reaction have been if she had told him that he had left her pregnant and alone, sick with grief, her love for him taking four years to bury? Even now . . .

She tore her mind away from useless speculation. Matt meant every word he had said, he had always had an edge of ruthlessness. It had only been with her that he had been gentle, tender.

Allan had been told that it would be another week before any decision would be made and she knew that this was Matt's cruelty, a cat-and-mouse game, with her as the mouse, while Matt watched with tawny-eyed amusement, waiting to make the kill.

She persuaded Allan to open his flat, telling him that she intended to take the girls to Yorkshire and show them the Dales. Again it would eat into her

meagre resources but she felt unable to simply sit and
wait for Matt to pronounce the death sentence. And
she could not tell Allan about her deep fears.

He had sworn that if he ever discovered the name
of the man who had left her ill, pregnant and in
despair, he would kill him. It was too dramatic now,
four years had passed, but he would only make things
worse and it would put her secret right into Matt's
hands. She was tied into a knot of her own making
and she would have to endure the guilt that she felt
on Allan's behalf for the rest of her life.

Carrie took the train to York, a new experience for
the twins, and hired a car to drive up into the Dales.
Allan had insisted on booking them into the Green
Man at Hetherage, a village a few miles away from
the place where he and Carrie had spent a happy
childhood. It was a pilgrimage to Grandma Ellie, to
the past. Carrie wanted to see no familiar faces, only
to breathe in the fresh, cold air of the north, to see
the sparkling shallow rivers, the distant sombre power
of the hills.

In the bright, cold air of the following day, she
stood on the high ground above Hawthorn Cottage.
It had been sold when her grandmother died, but even
now it looked exactly as it had always done. She could
see the herb garden she had helped to tend, the crazy-
paved path to the door, the bushes where sweet-
smelling roses would bloom in June.

The apple tree was still there, its old branches
looking as sturdy as they had been when she and
Allan had climbed it long ago. There was no sadness.
The twins raced through the short heather, an unaccustomed rosiness in their faces, rolling and scrambling
like two puppies in the freedom of the hills, while
Carrie looked long and hard at the scene, her mind
lingering on the very distant past as she let the peace

and the harsh beauty heal some of her wounds.

'Face up to today, Caroline. Tomorrow may never happen.' She could almost hear her grandmother's voice. But tomorrow had happened and would never go away.

Matt had come back into her life after Grandma Ellie's death and had changed her whole future. She looked back at Gemma and Pippa, their hair the cool gold of the northern sun, their eyes the same warm golden brown as the eyes of the man who had taken her life into his hands.

He had said goodbye after her birthday but it had never been goodbye even if he had meant it then. It had been during the following month that Grandma Ellie had died, peacefully and happily, and although Carrie went home for the funeral and cried with Allan's arm around her, her grandmother had left no sadness behind. She had lived her life happily, had made them happy, and now there remained only her carefully treasured possessions, her words of wisdom and her outrageous assumptions.

Carrie returned to Redland after the funeral, to hard work and the satisfaction of doing something really well, pushing Matthew Silver into the back of her mind until he too became only a wistful memory.

It was three months later that she was called to the office phone at college and stood with racing heart listening to the sound of the voice she would never forget.

'Caroline?'

For a second she couldn't answer and he spoke sharply. 'Caroline? Answer me, for God's sake!'

She had irritated him without even speaking and her timid, 'Hello, Mr Silver,' did nothing to improve his temper.

'Matt!' he grated impatiently. 'What are you doing now, and if you say that you're standing there answering the phone and then trail off into silence in that annoying little way of yours, I'll come over there and put you across my knee!'

He was barking at her, furious for some reason. She managed to gulp out that she had just finished her last lecture of the day before he interrupted.

'Stay there! I'll pick you up in fifteen minutes!'

The phone was slammed down before she could make any comment and she collected her books, walking out to sit on the low wall that surrounded the little square, her legs too shaky to hold her up.

He was there in ten minutes, his face so stern that she expected him to shake her. He didn't. He took her books and put them in the back of the car, helping her into the passenger seat and driving off without a word.

Outside London, he really let the car go, heading out into open country on a fast road until she glanced nervously at the speedometer.

'Where are we going?'

'Anywhere!' he snapped. 'And will you stop speaking like a frightened mouse?'

He suddenly slowed and pulled off the road, switching off the engine and turning to her angrily, his arm across the back of the seat, his whole body swung sideways, the better to glare at her head on.

'I called to see you and you weren't at that—house, nobody was! You weren't there at any time for over a week!'

'But . . . ' She had no idea what he was talking about, why he should be so angry with somebody he hardly knew.

'And stop trailing into silence like that!'

Suddenly, she was really annoyed herself. She had almost managed to stop thinking about him until he had come storming along today. He had no right to question her so savagely when she'd met him so briefly before.

'I'll speak exactly as I please and it's nothing to do

with you where I've been—Mr Silver!' She added that with considerable pleasure. 'For your information, I've been nowhere. I can't afford to go anywhere. You may despise the place where I live but it's all my grant will stretch to. Most other students are just as badly off, some worse. I don't suppose you've ever been short of money or hungry in your life!'

Her attack stunned him, left him looking at her in utter silence for a second, and she knew she'd gone too far. She hardly ever lost her temper but when she did, her tongue never seemed to know when to stop. They just sat staring at each other.

Then he said in a shocked and quiet voice, 'Are you hungry, Caroline?'

'No, I didn't mean that at all. I was making a point.'

'Loudly and clearly,' he observed wryly. 'I've received your message perfectly.' She looked down at her clenched hands not knowing what to say, feeling on the edge of tears.

'At the risk of another sharp reprimand,' he continued more quietly, 'you were not there. You were definitely away for a whole week.'

Understanding dawned and she looked up.

'But that was three months ago!'

'True!' His face was stiff and she knew it must be anger again. 'Where were you for a whole week in the middle of the term?'

'I went home. Grandma Ellie—died.'

The tears spilled over, not for any other reason than that she didn't want him to be angry again, and she only stiffened briefly when he pulled her into his arms, relaxing almost at once as his hand stroked through her curls.

'Oh, God! I'm really an unfeeling, interfering brute, aren't I?'

She shook her head against his jacket and he lifted her face, wiping it dry with his handkerchief and looking as she remembered him, his eyes smiling, warm.

'Want to tell me about it?'

She carefully extricated herself from his arms and sat back in her seat, her eyes still wet with tears.

'There's nothing to tell. She was old but she was never ill in her life and she just—died. I'm not unhappy about it because she did everything she wanted to do and she was a wonderful person.'

He looked at her intently, his face serious as he absorbed this piece of philosophy.

'She must have been. She did a wonderful job bringing you up.' He was smiling as he tilted her chin. 'Just in case you are hungry . . . just in case you're lying—proudly—let's have a slap-up meal!' He started the car and pulled out into the empty road.

'But I'm not dressed . . . '

This time her little habit didn't irritate him. This time he laughed.

'Oh, come, I'm fairly certain that you are. If you hadn't been, I'd surely have noticed.'

Her face flushed but he grinned so widely at her little gasp of outrage that she found herself laughing.

After that, Matt's car was often in the mean little street as he came to pick her up and his visits grew more frequent until she seemed to be with him constantly. He took her to the theatre, to restaurants, sightseeing around the city like a tourist until she was completely relaxed with him, confident in his company, sure of herself.

She kept a tight grip on her imagination, knowing that there was a woman who was still probably in his mind, but glad that he seemed to find some happiness in her company and counted her no threat at all. For some reason, he had taken her under his wing, probably because of her shyness, but perhaps also because he knew that the place where she lived was as alien to her as it was to him.

Whatever his reasons, she loved being with him, loved the now familiar tingle when their eyes met, the feel of his hand on her arm, missing him badly when he was away from London. Her face filled with delight when he returned and met her, smiling into her eyes as she listened with blissful happiness to the deep warm sound of his voice.

Knowing that she missed the country air, Matt took her on a picnic as soon as the weather turned hot. He arrived one Saturday dressed in jeans and an open-necked shirt, a bulging picnic basket in the boot of the car and whisked her off to the clean, windswept air of the cliffs by the sea, driving almost as far as Dover.

It was a secret day, a day out of time, nobody but the two of them for miles it seemed, and it came into her mind that she was hugging the reality of Matt to herself alone as if he too was a secret. Certainly she had never written to Allan about him, had never discussed him with Jenny. She had even stopped making any attempt to form friendships with the other girls at college because Matt filled her thoughts every day and every night. She lived in a dream about him and even Vivienne had stopped warning her about the dangers of being with him. There was no danger.

Matt too seemed to be wrapping her in a blanket of protective secrecy, never introducing her to anyone they met who clearly knew him. He would stop politely enough to talk, but his hand would come to her shoulder, his restlessness to step back into the small world they inhabited together finally becoming apparent even to the most determined acquaintances.

It suited Carrie only too well. She knew that he spent every spare minute with her now but although she refused to let herself dream, she couldn't contemplate any sort of life away from him.

It was Carrie who packed the basket later while Matt stretched out on the big rug, watching her lazily as she set about it with as much enjoyment as she had shown when it was unpacked.

'I feel like Mole.' She grinned across at him like an urchin, sitting back on her heels, her T-shirt and jeans making her look incredibly young.

'You're all the wrong colour for that.' He suddenly looked away from her and sat up abruptly. 'I'll put it in the car!' For no reason at all, he was cool, tight-lipped, and she watched him anxiously as he lifted the basket and walked to the car, slinging it into the boot with an almost savage carelessness.

She was avoiding his eyes when he came back, standing beside the rug, her eyes on the fork in her hand. 'I'm sorry, I missed out a fork. I thought that I'd . . . ' His hands came to her shoulders, jerking her forward, and she looked up startled and scared as he stared into her eyes.

'Damn the fork and damn your idiotic little habits and the way you make me feel!'

Before she had time to think she was tightly in his arms and his mouth came down harshly on her parted lips as he grasped a handful of her curls and lifted her face to his.

When he let her go, she just stared at him, trembling, terrified by the feelings that tore through her, unable to stop looking into his eyes, her own eyes wide open, her body frighteningly aware of him and her mind admitting what it had struggled to deny for so long. She loved him, utterly and completely. It was a feeling that she had never had before, glorious and frightening, leaving her totally vulnerable.

'Oh, Carrie!' He breathed her name in a deep, soft whisper and reached out for her, soothing her trembling body when she was back in the hard warmth of his arms. He began to kiss her slowly, gently, delicate little caresses that turned her fear into warm, excited pleasure. His hands moved beneath her soft shirt to stroke her back, his lips to tease her ear, her neck, until she stood on tiptoe, her arms finding their way around his neck, at first timidly and then tightly as he pulled her closer.

When he sank to the rug, taking her with him, she nestled in his arms, completely pliant and willing, disappointed when he lifted his head.

'Kiss me back, Carrie,' he begged huskily, his golden-brown eyes searching her face with a kind of wonder.

'I don't know how. How could I? I never went anywhere except with Allan and anyway, Grandma Ellie wouldn't have . . . '

'God bless Grandma Ellie,' he said thickly, his fingers gently teasing her lips open.

He taught her to kiss him, slowly and gently at first until there was a desperate feeling inside her, until her little gasp of shock had turned to little whimpers of desire. When his hand slid from the smooth, warm skin of her back to cover her breasts, she made no protest, her only reaction was one of urgent demand until he lay across her, pressing her into the soft wool of the rug, kissing her urgently.

'Do you realise that we shouldn't be here? Shouldn't be doing this?' His eyes were dark and burning as he looked down at her.

'Why? I love you, Matt. I think I've loved you since I first saw you.'

'Don't say that!' His hands gripped her tightly. 'What you're feeling is desire, feeling it for the first time in your life, and I have no business to make you feel it!'

'I'm sorry.' Tears filled her eyes and she shut them tightly.

'I know you don't want me to love you. I know you think that I'm a child, probably stupid too . . . ' Her body tossed relentlessly in an agony of misery, brushing his, and he gasped, coming down heavily on her, his hands gripping her face harshly.

'Don't do that!' he rasped, staring into her eyes,

brushing the tears away roughly. 'You have no idea where this is leading, what I'm feeling! You don't even know what you're feeling yourself! I'm crazy to feel like this about you. You may not know any better but I certainly do and I don't want attachments!'

She tried to turn away but he groaned like a man in pain, capturing her mouth with his to kiss her deeply and hungrily, holding her tightly to him.

'Damn you, Carrie,' he muttered against her lips. 'I don't want to feel like this! I don't want to feel anything for you! I wish I'd never seen you at all!'

For a long time, he simply looked at her, fighting some inner battle that seemed to be miles away from her. She hardly dared to breathe, so afraid of losing him that she would gladly have died at that moment right where she was, locked securely in his arms.

'Come on,' he said unsteadily after a while. 'It's getting dark and we've a long way to go.'

The return trip was silent, not with the companionable silence they had shared so many times before but with a deep brooding silence from Matt that told her it was all over.

'Are you all right, Carrie?' He sounded gentle and he was still calling her Carrie. It gave her the courage to look at him because she knew that it would be for the last time.

'Yes, I'm sorry, Matt.'

'For what? It's not your fault. It never has been. I broke into your life like a thief and now you're not the same, not so dewy-eyed and secure in your innocence.'

'I can't be innocent for ever,' she murmured quietly, looking at the street lamps with eyes blurred by tears. 'One day . . . '

'One day,' he agreed softly, turning her face with his open palm and smiling into her eyes, 'but not with someone like me, sweet Carrie.' He stroked his hand down her face gently. 'Don't ever lose that little habit you've got. I'll always remember the way your voice trails into silence, the way you look with clear wide eyes at a very mean world.' He opened the car door, getting out and walking with her to her own miserable door,standing to look down into her pale face.

'Matt!' She was filled with terror at parting from him.

'Take care,' he said tightly. 'Goodbye, Carrie.'

She cried herself to sleep feeling so ill, so unhappy the next day that she made no move to get out of bed. It was Sunday anyway and Jenny had already left for Wolverhampton before Carrie had returned the night before.

All day she couldn't eat, dropping into fitful dozing, waking to cry a little more, and it was not until after eight o'clock that she wearily had a warm bath and made herself a hot drink, sitting on the edge of the bed, her cup tightly clasped in her hands, her eyes staring at the floor.

She nearly dropped the cup at the knock on the door. It was the first time that anybody had ever knocked and she knew it couldn't be Jenny. Everything that Matt had warned her of about this neighbourhood rushed through her mind but when the knock came again, sharp and impatient, she opened the door.

'How did you know it was me?' Matt stood there looking deathly, his face white, his shining hair tousled.

'I didn't. How could I?'

'But you opened the damned door! How many times do I have to tell you . . . '

His own voice faded away as he saw her face clearly, her wide eyes red from endless weeping, her trembling lips.

'Come for a drive,' he said abruptly.

'It's nearly nine.' She stood in her dressing-gown, clutching her drink. 'I'm—I'll have to get dressed.'

'Then get dressed, or come as you are, but, for God's sake come!'

She came. She shut him out while she pulled on her jeans and a soft woollen sweater, locking the door under his supervising stare and following him into the car.

He never spoke to her at all. He just drove down to the river and sat staring at the water, Carrie beside him too miserable to make conversation. What was there to say?

After half an hour of silence, when the warmth of the car slowly faded away and the chill of the river began to penetrate the closed-in luxury, she shivered and he looked round at her.

'I'll take you back.' He seemed to notice everything, and she didn't even nod her agreement. She had been no use to him, no help whatever and all that had happened was that her own misery had deepened.

His silence was too hurtful for words and when he stopped outside her door, she was frantic to get out and hide herself away.

'Carrie!' The desperate plea in his voice stopped her even before his hand reached her arm and they were staring into each other's eyes, pain on both their faces.

'Come with me, Carrie,' he begged softly. 'Pack your things and come with me.'

She fell into his arms and he held her as if he would never let her go, his lips against the tear-wet skin of her face.

'I've tried, Carrie. Oh, God, I've tried, but I'm slowly dying without you. I can't eat, I can't sleep, I can't work. I've got to have you close to me every minute. Don't cry any more, my darling.'

'Oh, Matt! I want to be with you. I'll never want anything else.' She was sobbing with happiness, her arms clinging to him and he turned her face up to his with anxious urgency.

'Do you know what I'm asking you, Carrie? I'm

not offering you the spare room in my flat. I want you to come with me, live with me, be my love.'

It was the most beautiful thing she had ever heard and her face turned for his kisses but he drew back, still uncertain.

'I'm not attempting to fool you, Carrie. I can't marry you, not yet. I can't commit myself to marriage but I want you now. I want you with me every day, in my arms every night and I know it's selfish and I've no right to ask you.'

He was kissing her then, holding her close, healing the great wound of yesterday, bringing her back to life, and she didn't care about anything but being with Matt, she knew it was for ever.

He helped her to pack, to leave a message for Jenny and a pile of crisp notes for the rent, hers and Jenny's, and then she was back in the car, her head against his shoulder, speeding through the darkened streets her heart singing.

In the unaccustomed luxury of his flat she was a little frightened. It was all so new, only Matt familiar, and he watched her sombrely, torment on his face as she prowled the huge sitting-room like a trapped kitten.

'I'll take you back, Carrie,' he said after a while, his voice flat and empty but she looked at him and stood still.

'If I can't be with you, then I don't want to be anywhere. I love you, Matt.' Her eyes fell before the blaze in his and he walked softly towards her, tilting her face to the light.

'You really mean it, don't you?' he asked in a sort of wonder.

'Yes, Matt. I meant it yesterday but you didn't believe me.' She looked up into his gleaming eyes and he stroked her face, examining every feature.

'I was too scared to believe it. It meant too much

to me. You're frightened, Carrie? You think that I'll hurt you?'

'No.' She shook her head, her eyes smiling into his. 'It's just that it's new and . . . ' He hugged her close, his lips against her hair, rocking her protectively in his arms.

'If I ever lose you, Carrie,' he whispered, 'I think it will kill me. I've never felt like this before in my life. The way I feel about you is utterly overwhelming and so beautiful that it scares me.'

He lifted her into his arms, his lips closing over hers as he carried her from the room. His lovemaking was an adoration, an act of worship binding her to him for ever, her name a lingering melody on his lips as she fell into a deep and dreamless sleep in his arms.

CHAPTER THREE

GEMMA'S tug on her jacket, the quiet little voice, brought her back to the fact that she was cold, had been standing staring straight ahead for ages.

'I'm hungry, please.' The beautiful little eyes looked into hers and Carrie picked her up, hugging her close before going to fetch Pippa to return to the hotel and the bleak present.

She phoned Allan in the afternoon and the dullness of his voice told her that he knew his fate at last.

'Can you come back, Carrie?' He sounded completely defeated. 'I just can't talk to you on the phone. I know you planned a week up there but honestly, I need to talk to you, to sort out some kind of future for all of us. For now, we'll squeeze into my flat and then during the week we'll look for something a bit bigger, a bit cheaper too, probably.'

'I'll be there in the morning.'

It was too far to drag the girls all the way back that night, but she was on the road by seven the next day and a fast, early train got her into London in good time. She was in the flat by noon, the twins fed and having a quick nap by one.

'You heard the result?' As soon as they were alone she tackled the subject and Allan nodded, slumped dejectedly into a chair.

'I got the letter yesterday. All support withdrawn and they're wanting to get back as much as they can. They'd take everything I had—if I had anything. The letter was from that chap Silver, on behalf of Carter-Rousseau, but it's damned clear that it's on behalf of himself. They've just let him do everything and, oh boy, has he done everything! In the past few days, he's gone through the affairs of Croft Computers like a whirlwind. I'm not even to be given another chance to speak to him. He has spoken!'

He wanted to discuss the immediate future, the plans he had to take care of Carrie and the girls, the possibility of a job in industry for himself to tide them over the bad times, but Carrie hardly heard. She was bitterly angry, in a cold rage at the way that Matt had punished Allan because of her. Her deep affection for Allan, her gratitude, her wild anger at the injustice of it all had her making an excuse to leave the flat in the middle of the afternoon. Twenty minutes later, a taxi deposited her at the imposing entrance of the company offices of Silver Electronics.

'I want to see Mr Silver!' There would be no 'I would like to', 'May I . . . ?', 'Can Mr Silver spare me a minute?' and the startled receptionist was calling Matt's office before she had really given the matter much thought.

'A Mrs Haley would like to see you, sir.' She looked a little anxious but Matt's voice came immediately on the line, satisfaction, grim amusement in every word.

'I'm expecting her. Send her up.'

Expecting her! Yes, he probably was. Expecting her to plead, to weep, but she knew that was useless. She had seen the cold cruelty on his face the other night, had seen the icy, merciless eyes. Pleading would be useless and that was not why she was here. Their ship was sunk, Allan's and hers, but before she left Matt Silver's life finally, he would know what she thought of him.

He had a new office, not the one she had visited with him, and all the staff she saw were new, even his secretary, the kindly, comfortable Rosemary replaced by a woman in a black suit and rimless spectacles. It seemed he surrounded himself nowadays with people as cold as himself, stiff faced, metallic automatons.

She barely spared the secretary a glance, storming into Matt's private office and closing the door in the startled face of the woman who looked too efficient to be human.

The office gave her a momentary shock. It seemed to measure about a half-acre, modern, stark and utterly unlike Matt's former place. He was sitting at a huge rosewood desk and he remained seated, his eyes glinting with the cold humour of a god who had crushed a planet to amuse himself.

'You're late, Mrs Haley. A whole day late. I expected you yesterday, right after the delivery of the morning post, or didn't the letter arrive until today?' He lit a dark cheroot and leaned back. 'Plead away, then! I'm surprised that you have the intelligence to realise that I can still put a stop to the havoc.'

He was enjoying this, cruelly and calmly watching her, waiting for her to sob out pleas, to be utterly beaten.

'No doubt you could put a stop to it,' she exclaimed bitterly, marching to the desk, her eyes stormy, 'but I know you have no such intention. And I'm not here to plead, Mr Silver! I didn't plead when you left me. I didn't weep all the way to Florida and arrive on my knees. I simply left in the other direction. I've come to tell you that I have a contempt for you that goes too deep for words. It's alarming to imagine that I once imagined myself in love with such a monster. You were right, it should never have been someone like you, as I found out later.'

His eyes had narrowed at her reference to Florida and her clear intimation that marriage to Kevin Haley had shown her what real love was all about, but his recovery was so swift that she might well have imagined the look that had flared across his face.

'I see you've lost that little habit of trailing into silence,' he interrupted softly, his eyes moving over her with no interest whatever. 'Let me set matters clearly in front of you before you waste any more valuable breath. I have every intention of stopping the havoc. Your cousin is a very clever man, brilliant even. If you had told me when you were—living with me,' he continued, his eyes holding hers coldly, 'if you had thought to mention your adored cousin more deeply, he would have had no struggle at all. In those days you only had to whisper a secret wish to me and it was a command. I haven't grown rich by sinking valuable businesses and Croft Computers is a winner. The letter was, shall we say, a sharp call to heel, a hard snap of the leash. Carter-Rousseau are waiting for a call from me that will put your cousin back in business in comfort without the need to half kill himself tearing all over Australia.'

She was too stunned to think clearly, wanting to sit down—on the floor if necessary.

'Then why have you let matters go so far? Why, if you intend to save the firm have you . . . ?'

'Ah! The elusive habit. Taken the wind out of your sails, have I?' He stood slowly, stubbing out the cheroot before looking up at her with eyes narrowed and cold. 'I've let it go so far to show you that I mean every word I say, to show you precisely how the deck is stacked. My call to Carter-Rousseau can be a yes or a no. If I say no, the receiver will be in before the week is over, winding up a nice little firm that I shall then gobble up and incorporate with Silver Electronics. There is a condition to fulfil before I say yes and save Croft Computers, leaving your cousin on the way to being a wealthy man himself.'

'A condition?' It was all too much for her, because nothing was going as she had imagined. She should be happy, relieved, but Matt's icy face warned her not to be any such thing. 'What condition? Allan can't do any more for the firm. He can't work harder! What can he do to meet any condition?'

'Not your cousin, Mrs Haley—you!' He looked at
her with cruel satisfaction, seeing all the fight in her
ebbing away into bewilderment and unease. 'I'll save
Croft Computers providing that you meet the necessary condition. I want you back!'

She stared at him, white to the lips and the room
began to spin, to darken as she clutched at the desk
to save herself, dimly hearing him call her name before
she let her grip on the day slide away.

When she opened her eyes seconds later, she was in
the security of a big leather chair, Matt trickling cool
water between her bloodless lips, his hand behind her
head. She looked at him blankly, disorientated for a
brief while but reality returning speedily to make her
shrink away from his touch.

He straightened and walked back to lean against
his desk, simply watching her like a tawny-eyed cat
again.

'I see you don't like the idea of a fate worse than
death,' he said coldly, his own face pale. 'You have a
good line in making a point strongly.'

'You're out of your mind,' she whispered when her
trembling lips would allow her to speak.' Do you
imagine I'll go through all that again? I've got two
children!'

'I really was never aware that living with me had
been such an ordeal for you,' he remarked quietly and
sardonically. 'You should have mentioned it at the
time and I could have set you up in a luxury flat of
your own and only visited you for fatherly talks and
to look at you. I was sufficiently besotted with you to
do almost anything you asked. The fact that you have
two children has not escaped my notice either,' he
grated harshly. 'I want the whole package, you and
the twins, but this time it's permanent, there'll be no
wandering off into the great never-never land.'

He reached into his pocket and placed a piece of
paper on the desk, his eyes never leaving hers.

'A special licence on your left, a telephone on your right. You'll agree to marry me or I pick up that phone and your cousin is finished.'

'Why are you doing this?' She was watching him in real horror, her mind refusing to see any future where she would be in the power of someone whose hatred showed so clearly on his face.

'Nobody take me for a ride,' he said with deadly quiet. 'Nobody even tries, but you, you succeeded and now you pay. I have no hold whatever over you and you've proved yourself to be a scheming little bitch even at nineteen. However, I do have a hold over your much-loved cousin—a stranglehold! It's all in the family, Caroline, and one of you picks up the tab.'

'You're hateful, cruel . . .'

'You've met a present-day Viking! How surprised Grandma would have been.'

'I won't do it!' She sprang to her feet, his mention of Grandma Ellie putting some life into her.

He never turned a hair. Instead he lifted the phone.

'Goodbye, Allan,' he mocked softly, his eyes filled with malice. 'Hallo? Get me Carter-Rousseau on the line.'

'Wait!' She sprang forward, her hand on his sleeve and he looked down at it with cool amusement.' I've got to think! I've got to have time to think about it!'

'Cancel the call,' he said quietly into the phone before replacing it gently on the rest. 'You have until this evening to think. You will ring me at the flat. I imagine you can remember the number, you lived there once—with me. If by seven o'clock I have not heard from you, I'll roust the chairman out of his warm sitting-room and finish the necessary demolition before I go to bed.' He lifted the phone again. 'Call a taxi for Mrs Haley.' It seemed that nowadays he never said please or thank you. He only issued orders.

'Goodbye for now, Caroline,' he said smoothly, sitting back behind his desk, leaving her standing on trembling legs. 'A nice quiet wedding, I think, with a champagne lunch to follow, nothing flashy or extravagant, all in the family.'

'What about the girls?' she whispered, her eyes dark and shocked.

'You want them at the wedding?' His eyebrows rose sardonically and she shook her head defeatedly.

'Of course not. I meant, what will people say? What will they think?'

'People?' His eyes scorched her with dislike.' People asked where you were. People looked surprised, pitying! *People* will be told that you were ill for a long time, even before the twins were born, but now, you're all better!' His lips were one hard line. 'My friends won't question things, they actually liked you. Nobody else will dare!'

'The girls are called Haley,' she muttered, her eyes falling before his cold anger.

'Temporarily!' he snapped. 'To the world, to—people —they're mine. They'll cope easily enough. Little girls soon forget, Caroline. You did!'

'You've got it all worked out, haven't you?' she accused, her eyes, the whole of her body defeated.

'To the last full stop,' he assured her. 'Until this evening then, Caroline, when I just know you'll ring me. Your devotion to the unfortunate cousin is so obvious. Look at it this way, you'll be setting him up for life.'

'And what about me?' she whispered.

'You've obviously got one wonderful person in your cousin. From the look in your eyes when you spoke about Haley, you had another one there. Don't expect a third. You had plenty of things when you lived with me and the things I gave you were given in love. Now it will be my duty, but neither you nor the girls will suffer materially and as to the children, I think I would probably have made a good father. I'll now get the chance to practice.'

The phone rang and he picked it up. 'Silver!'

She was dismissed and the steps that had stormed into the office, to face him in the cold luxury now dragged defeatedly out again as she went down to the taxi he had ordered.

Before the taxi dropped her at Allan's flat she had managed to regain some measure of composure. The girls were still asleep and the realisation hit her like a hard blow. She had changed the course of all their lives while the twins had a short nap. It had seemed like a whole day.

'Sit down.' Allan had turned easily as she came in but now he was alert and watchful, his eyes on her pale face. 'Better tell me now, Carrie. I can see that something has really shaken you.'

She told him, but at first he couldn't seem to take it in.

'Just a minute.' He sat down himself. 'You're getting married to Matt Silver—the—Matt Silver, Silver Electronics? But, my crazy girl, you only met him the other night and you've been in Yorkshire ever since.' He looked dejected. 'Obviously I'm in the dark completely or you're having a brainstorm.'

There was no way that she could avoid telling him about the bargain and he was on his feet, eyes blazing in a second.

'The swine! You'll do no such thing! You know I won't let you. You're crazy if you think I'll hand you and the girls over to a complete stranger—who seems to be a lunatic. God, he's only seen you the once!'

'I know Matt, Allan,' she said quietly. 'I know Matt better than anyone, even better than I know you, at least, I used to think I knew him.'

He watched her silently, more stunned by the impossibility of it than by anything else now.

'You'll not be handing the girls over to a stranger, Allan,' she added, unable to keep anything a secret now. 'You'll be handing them over to their father. Matt and I . . . '

'So he's the one!' He was on his feet again, making for the door and she had to spring up to stop him.

'Wait! Don't go rushing off like a madman, Allan. Hear out the whole story. It ended badly but it didn't begin like that. At first it was wonderful, the happiest time of my life, and Matt has no idea that Gemma and Pippa belong to him. After the way he left me, after the way he treated me, I'll never tell him.'

'You can tell him to drop dead! I'll tell him myself!' He was off again but this time she stopped him finally and quietly.

'I want to marry him, Allan. As far as he's concerned, nobody knows about this but him and me and he's got it all worked out. If you told him about the twins it would only be another knife for him to cut me with and he has enough of those already. However you feel, you must keep quiet about that. Of course, he'll realise that I will tell you about the past, but the twins are my secret, Allan. I'm marrying Matt for other reasons than to save the firm.' She was astounded at her ability to lie so smoothly even to Allan. If Grandma Ellie could see her now! 'The girls are his. He's wealthy and he wants to take us all on. Let him! I promise you, he'll pay for walking out on me and he'll pay for this unjust attack on you, but the twins have a wealthy father, they're heirs to millions, it's their right.'

'And it's your life!' He knelt in front of her and took her cold hands in his. 'You deserve happiness, not daily battle. Carrie, love, reconsider. The hell with the firm! I'll start again.'

'Why should you?' Her eyes suddenly came to blazing life. 'He intends to gobble up the firm, to use all your ideas and set it up on its feet for himself. His words, Allan! I have a score to settle on my own account and the girls' future to consider.'

'Suppose you meet someone else, want to marry?'

'I never will. In the whole world I trust only you—Matt saw to that. We shall all prosper at his expense and every day I'll repay him blow for blow.'

'Why are you kneeling in front of Mummy, Uncle Allan?' Pippa came out of the bedroom rubbing sleepy eyes but very interested.

'We're practising a play.' His wit was ever ready and Pippa came forward eagerly.

'Can I be in it?'

'Certainly, take up your position.'

Carrie's eyes filled with tears as she looked at him, smiling.

'I don't know how I'll ever manage without you, Allan.'

'You'll never have to,' he growled. 'That'll be the day!' But she knew she would have to. She was walking into Matt's plans like a human sacrifice and she doubted her ability to repay his savagery. The past was too firmly locked in her heart.

In the privacy of Allan's bedroom, she phoned Matt later saying just two words.

'I agree.'

He was equally brief. 'Good! The wedding's on Friday.'

'But you can't! Today is Tuesday, there's no time, it's not possible!'

'Consider it settled.' His voice was cold and hard even over the phone, not even a lingering trace of the deep, quiet warmth that had been Matt. 'I can pull strings and I can lean on people. Friday is the day. Tomorrow I'll pick you up for dinner and we'll discuss the wedding and the future.

'There's no future,' she said bleakly.

'Wrong, Mrs Haley! There is a long, long future and it begins on Friday. Give me your address.'

'I'll meet you. I don't want you here. I'll get a taxi to your office, or anywhere!'

'Your address, Caroline! I'll pick you up.' She gave in, she always had done with Matt, and it didn't even seem to give him satisfaction. He expected it.

He wasn't driving the Ferrari, he came in a sombre black Mercedes and she raced down to meet him as soon as she saw him step out. The way Allan felt, there was a strong possibility that he would go for Matt the moment he opened the door of the flat. He had been sworn to secrecy about the twins but she knew that he was raging inside, hurting for her, only going along with her plans because she insisted.

She had to comment on the car when Matt simply handed her into that dark interior and pulled out into the traffic.

'The Ferrari? I grew out of it. You'll find that I've grown out of most things. For example, I'm not in the least indulgent, not any more.'

Neither was she. She sat in stony silence, the bright glitter of the hotel passing completely over her head. She was not nineteen any more and it would take more than bright lights to worry her. She was facing a future of bleak misery and Matt's cruel little trick of bringing her to dine here was a waste of his time. She sat silently and ate her meal methodically, leaving all the talking to him.

'Have you taken all that in?' he rasped in an annoyed voice when his meticulous details for the wedding morning had received only brief nods from her.

'I have. A car will collect me at nine-thirty to get me to St Andrew's church for ten. The wedding will be over by ten-thirty when we go to the Savoy for an early champagne lunch. We collect the twins and go—home. Have I missed anything out?'

'Not a thing,' he growled, watching her angrily. 'You've not enquired, of course, where home is to be.'

'Does it matter?'

'To me, no, but I like to have everything in order. We'll be living at Falconridge. Ruby is back there getting it ready.'

When she merely nodded, drinking her wine and looking idly round the room, he slapped a card on the table from one of the major banks, following it with a cheque book in a leather case.

'There's your cheque book and credit card. I've opened an account for you in your maiden name. After the wedding I'll get it changed.'

For a second she stared at the stiff plastic card. Caroline Stuart. She was still that, but over four years of pretence, years of being Mrs Haley, had practically driven her own name from her mind.

'Why do I need this?'

'You'll need clothes. Get anything you need for yourself and the children. Spend it in any damned way you like!'

'I have clothes, thank you. I'll not arrive at the church either naked or in black.' She pushed the cheque book towards him but he pushed it back firmly his mouth twisting unexpectedly into the semblance of a smile.

'You've developed a sharp edge, Caroline,' he noted quietly. 'I appreciate your reluctance but the account is yours permanently. Consider it to be an ever-full pot.'

'Very well.' She picked up both items and slid them into her bag. 'You have now bought a wife. This week's bargain, congratulations. With this first purchase you are entitled to a pair of identical twins.'

He was on his feet, towering over her, his fingers like hot steel biting into her wrist as he pulled her to her feet, his eyes blazing.

'And don't you ever forget it, Mrs Haley!' he ground out savagely. 'I've bought you, lock, stock and barrel, twins included. After Friday I have a family of three and one seriously irritated cousin-in-law. You may be a restless and unwilling wife, but that is is exactly what you will be—*my wife!*'

He marched her out to the car, slamming the door on her, and was settling grimly behind the wheel before she had the breath to reply.

'If you imagine that I'll be a wife, if you imagine that I'll . . . '

'Sleep with me?' He turned to look at her like a man made of stone.' Don't distress yourself. I've made my reasons very plain. You are marrying me to set the record straight, to close a file marked "Where the hell is Carrie?" As to the other, I grew out of the past. I abandoned it with the red Ferrari. You'll live in ordered luxury, you will look after the children, you will accompany me to any function that requires a dutiful wife and you'll sleep alone with your beautiful memories of Mr Haley!'

He pulled out into the street, not speaking again until he stopped outside Allan's flat to drop her off.

'Does this doting relative of yours know that he's going to give you away on Friday?'

'He will not! His only desire is to seriously maim you. He's going along with this because I've told him that I'll do it whether he likes it or not, but he'll not come to see me married to someone he'd like to kill!'

'Very well, John Carmichael can stand in for him,' Matt said quietly, referring to the company lawyer of Silver Electronics. 'And why will you do it whether he likes it or not, Caroline?' he added softly.

'I have twin daughters, two little girls without a father and I have no money worth speaking of. You plotted and planned to marry me. Well, it suits me fine. You have more than enough money for all of us.' She played her trump card with what she hoped was a cruelty to match his own and she hit the mark, his eyes narrowed to points of ice.

'Yes, the twins. Don't forget that on Friday they become my daughters!'

'They'll call you Uncle, just like they call Allan Uncle!' she retorted sharply.

'They'll call me Daddy!' he ground out, his hand hard on her chin. 'I may have to spend the rest of my life seeing you look over your shoulder, seeing you all misty-eyed about the lost Mr Haley, but I'll damned well not watch two children follow in your path!'

'I'll not let you wipe out Kevin's memory!' She played it to the full, seeing instinctively a weak spot and striking as hard as she could to obliterate her own hurt.

'For you, I wouldn't even try! I'm just not interested, but I'll not see the children with that kind of albatross around their necks. On Friday, I collect those girls and they call me Daddy!'

'They know their name is Haley. How can I explain?' she pleaded, trying to extricate herself from the hard grip on her chin.

'I'll do that. I'm sure I can satisfy the minds of two babies. Just see that you go along with it or I'll think up some punishment that will make that curly hair stand on end!'

CHAPTER FOUR

CARRIE felt that she had been hit by a hurricane, and she had only Thursday to prepare for the arrival of Matt into her life. When she had been part of his life before, he had been another person, and this new Matt was an unfeeling stranger who scared her and who was one jump ahead of her in every move she made.

Her greatest concern was how he would react to the twins. To stand in a crowded room and tell him that they were three and a half was easy enough, but living with them daily, would he notice that they were older? A few months made little difference in the life of an adult but a small child could develop rapidly in that time. It seemed almost possible sometimes actually to see them grow and mature. Gemma and Pippa would be four at the beginning of June and she had no idea how to even begin getting herself out of that fix.

It was very cold on Friday and she was glad of her choice of clothes, a pale grey suit with matching shoes. At one time she had imagined herself as a dreamy bride in white, standing beside Matt on their wedding day, but she hadn't known then that she was only a temporary obsession. Now, the longed-for day was merely a punishment, merely to close a file.

When the car came, she stared at Allan, her heart thumping with fright, and his great hug was the only thing that kept her going as the car threaded its way through the traffic. She had not dared to show any fear to Allan; he was waiting, poised to cancel the whole thing, poised to tear round to Matt and offer physical violence. This time, she really was on her own if she didn't want everything collapsing around her ears.

John Carmichael was waiting for her outside the church, looking oddly out of place and owlish in his horn-rimmed spectacles and morning suit.

'Caroline. It's good to see you back, my dear. You're looking well.'

He was clearly glad to see her and he was a friendly face at least, possibly the person that she and Matt had seen most of in their time together.

'Your—your bouquet, my dear.' He looked embarrassed, his face a little pink as he dived round the corner of the porch and produced the flowers. Carrie stood completely stunned. An exquisite spray of violets, a cascade of beautifully arranged flowers caught together with delicate silver leaves among the natural green.

'Matt had me pick these up on the way. They'd been making them up for hours, they grumbled no end. It's typical of Matt. Apparently he went in and said exactly what he wanted on Wednesday morning, even drew a sketch. These silver leaves had to be specially made, it's real silver, you know, and they couldn't fix the flowers until the jeweller . . . well, you know Matt!' he finished awkwardly, giving his spectacles a push on to his nose.

She was glad that he'd rambled on because she didn't know what to think. Flowers had never entered her mind. They added a reality to the wedding, a thing so small to make it almost beautiful. 'Eyes like violets.' She was glad he couldn't see her now. What would he have said? 'Taken the wind out of your sails, have I?'

And when she entered the small church, clutching tightly to John Carmichael's arm, expecting to meet a cold empty building on a dismal March day, her steps faltered. The church was full, friends and acquaintances of Matt's who knew her and had accepted her readily. The organ played and the whole place blazed with imported blooms.

It seemed later that she had heard nothing of the ceremony. She wasn't even sure if she had answered at the right time but she must have done because the words, 'I now pronounce you man and wife,' had Matt turning to her and taking her in his arms but what to the whole congregation appeared to be a gentle kiss on her cheek, was really Matt's whisper in her ear, 'Now they can close their file. Now they know where Carrie is.'

It had her stiffening, had her momentary feeling of warmth and security fading into anxiety. She was now fully trapped, half of an impossible bargain, security for Allan's future. No more to Matt than the ultimate filing of a piece of paper.

Somehow she got through the brief but colourful reception, somehow she kept a smile fixed on her face. Matt had the whip hand and she knew that if she stumbled in any way in their presentation of a happy couple reunited, his retaliation would be both swift and ruthless, probably aimed at Allan.

He calmly mounted the steps to Allan's flat beside her later as they went to collect the twins. Carrie had no idea whether she would have to face a violent scene. Only the presence of the girls would prevent it, she knew, and she would dearly have liked to order Matt to stay in the car, but nobody ordered Matt to do anything. In any case, Allan would have to face working in some way with Matt and it would be better to get everything over with at once.

The sound of her key in the door had obviously brought Allan to his feet, the girls were nowhere to be seen and his face was filled with cold rage as he looked at Matt.

'If you harm her, if in any way you hurt Carrie or the girls, I'll . . . '

'She was mine once,' Matt interrupted with a quiet decisiveness. 'I've merely recovered her. As to the twins, rest easy, I have a very soft spot for children.'

Knowing that it was a deep dig at her again, Carrie bit her lip, hardly daring to breathe. They were like two gladiators and she wondered how she could ever have imagined that her sacrifice would put things right.

'You and I will be forced to work together for some little time,' Matt continued coldly, his height seeming to fill the doorway. 'It's part of the ground rules laid down by Carter-Rousseau. I therefore suggest that we let things lie for a few days and then begin in a civilised manner. As my cousin-in-law you can hate away as much as you like. As the nominal head of Croft Computers, I'll expect total co-operation and normal good manners.'

Any reply from Allan was stifled as the twins came into the room and Carrie hurried forward to clutch them to her in a protective gesture that was not lost on Matt.

'Get their things and let's go!' he ordered briefly.

'Where are we going, Mummy?' Pippa's clear voice held no worries and her eyes sought Matt's fearlessly.

'We're going home,' Matt answered before Carrie could speak. 'It's cold today so you'll need your coats. Did you pack their things?' he added for Carrie, but she only nodded.

'I want Uncle Allan to come,' Pippa said in her firm, determined way, but Matt's voice was just as firm.

'Uncle Allan lives here, but he'll see you as often as he likes to come to our house.' It was a clear message to Allan to toe the line or be cut completely out of the twins' lives.

She thought Allan would explode, but Gemma saved the day.

'Will I like it, though?' There was the usual thread

of anxiety in her voice and Matt came into the room, invited or not, to lift Carrie bodily away and crouch in front of the twins, his eyes on Gemma.

'I think you will. It's a big house in the country and there's a river with swans. I think you'll like it but if you don't, we can easily get another house to live in.'

'I might like it,' Gemma said hurriedly, hedging her bets, and Matt nodded.

'We'll give it a few weeks' try.'

Gemma seemed satisfied but Carrie suddenly felt a desperate urgency to get out. Any moment and Pippa was going to demand to know who Matt was, she could see it brewing up on her face, and Carrie had not told Allan about this part of the bargain. Even now she felt sure he would be holding down the scathing things he wanted to ram down Matt's throat about his treatment of her and then her subterfuge would be over.

She brought out the suitcases she had packed the night before and Matt took them from her.

'Bring the girls,' he ordered tersely before turning to look at Allan. 'I'll be in touch during the next few days. Until then do nothing except think! Your ideas are brilliant, keep them strictly on computing and leave my family to adjust to a new life.'

He had gone before Allan could reply and Carrie hurried forward to hug him.

'God, Carrie! Why did you agree?'

'Shh! Let it rest. I know Matt and we're not beaten yet.' Brave words bravely spoken but she knew who was in control and deep down, so did Allan.

She moved to sit in the back of the car with the twins but once again, Matt put her bodily aside, leaning in to tuck a warm rug across their legs as they sat like two angels on the huge seat. This little luxury moved them firmly in his direction and, with a quick grin into their pleased faces, he put Carrie into the passenger seat in a no-nonsense manner.

They were well out of London and travelling in smooth silence when the quiet was broken, oddly enough, not by Pippa.

'I'm hungry, please!' Gemma's quiet protest had Carrie spinning round guiltily.

'Oh, darling! I forgot that it's past lunchtime.' She felt a pretty hopeless mother but Matt took it all in his stride.

'Here, I think.' He swung off the road to a small hotel set well back in the trees, and Carrie gave him a small look of gratitude but his eyes were only on the twins as he turned to look at them.

'What would you really like to eat?'

He was instantly overwhelmed with requests and he and a highly amused waitress put together a menu that would have satisfied a horse. The twins settled to eat hungrily while Carrie and Matt sat with drinks and watched them, Matt with the first sign of warm amusement on his face that Carrie had seen since they had met again.

And finally it came, Pippa's question. When she was sufficiently full to allow for a pause, she looked steadily at Matt.

'Are you Uncle Matt, like we have Uncle Allan?'

Carrie held her breath but Matt said smoothly, 'Of course not, I'm your daddy!' He sounded so surprised that Pippa was silent, but only momentarily.

'We don't have a daddy any more, we never saw him, he went away.'

'I had to be away. They don't like me in Australia and you had to help Uncle Allan, didn't you?'

After a little thought, Pippa nodded. 'Why don't they like you?'

'Ah! It's my name.' Matt leaned forward and lowered his voice. 'You're not allowed to be called Silver in Australia and that's why you had to be called another name. You'd better both remember now that your name is really Silver.'

'Why can't you be called Silver?' Pippa asked excitedly, really intrigued, her voice lowered to imitate Matt's conspiracy.

'Well, it seems that there was once an outlaw called that and . . . '

'Like Ned Kelly!' Pippa interrupted triumphantly, digging out the name from her fund of knowledge gained from Allan's wild stories.

'Exactly!' She and Matt seemed to be deeply locked in the wonder of it all and Carrie glanced quickly at Gemma who had come to stand at Matt's side, her lunch abandoned, her hand on his knee.

'Am I Gemma Silver?'

Matt nodded, his face softening remarkably.

'Is it a good idea, though?' He smiled into her anxious little face and lifted her on to his knee.

'It's a brilliant idea!' he assured her softly and Carrie had to agree. Matt's fairy tales matched Allan's any day. 'Isn't it good that we can all be together again?' he added, smoothing the flaxen hair from around Gemma's face. 'Daddy's going to really love being with you all at last.'

She was satisfied and spun round quickly to look when he added softly, 'There's a duck on the grass outside that window.' There was, and both girls were scrambling to get to the window and look.

'Leave them,' he ordered as Carrie would have intervened. 'They've got to let that information sink in slowly. For now, a duck takes precedence.'

'I hope . . . ' She felt uneasy at voicing her thoughts but Matt insisted.

'Out with it, Caroline! What do you hope?'

'I hope you're not going to spoil Gemma,' she said anxiously. 'They've got to be treated alike and you seem to . . . '

He looked at her steadily.

'Pippa and I understand each other,' he said quietly. 'She doesn't scare. In a few years' time she'll be standing up to me with her chin sticking out and her eyes blazing.' He looked across at the twins, his eyes thoughtful. 'Gemma needs reassuring, she always will, I think. She reminds me of somebody I used to know.'

He never looked at Carrie, he didn't need to; clearly, he saw the close resemblance between Gemma's character and her own when she had met him and she fervently hoped that he didn't see what she had always seen, Pippa was her father's daughter and there was no mistaking that.

'I've got a soft spot for Gemma already,' he said quietly, 'but I'll try not to spoil her too much and you can stop worrying, Carrie, they'll be treated just as if they were my own children.'

He was looking at her coolly, and no doubt the fact that he had called her Carrie was a mere slip of the tongue. It didn't alarm her. What did alarm her was the quick burst of happiness it gave her.

By the time they reached Falconridge, the day had sunk into a threatening darkness that the early chill had promised. The big gates at the end of the drive stood open already and Matt grunted his satisfaction that he wouldn't have to get out and see to them. There was rain in the air and the dismal day took all the colour out of the great stretch of parkland that surrounded the house.

The gardens too were a sad ghost of their normal glory, but Carrie saw them with eyes that had seen the blaze of colour that would soon fill them. Very soon, the daffodils would be out, a great yellow carpet under the trees, already she could see them, and she found her eyes tracing the remembered clusters of plants, her mind filling the gardens with colour. She had been so happy here that it was almost impossible to look at the place without a smile, even though the smile would be wistful.

The old Regency house looked just the same, perfect and beautiful, and Matt brought the car to a halt by the long flight of shallow steps.

'Home, girls,' he said quietly to the twins. 'Come and see if you're going to like it.' He was speaking to them but his eyes were on Carrie for a moment, his expression watchful and guarded, and she looked swiftly away, hoping that her pleasure had not shown on her face. It was not the same now, the house had once been filled with the warmth of their love. Now it was going to be a luxurious prison for her, and she had better keep that fact permanently in mind.

She lingered though when Matt took the girls up the steps and opened the door, her eyes scanning the lawns across to the river. Today it looked angry, swollen with spring rains, but it would soon be murmuring on gently, its quiet music filling the bedroom at night. She stiffened as Matt's hand came on her arm, her face tightening. She would be in another bedroom, not Matt's.

'Come inside. It's cold out here and anyway, Ruby will be wanting to see you, she always was your devoted fan.'

His face gave away nothing and she tried to match his indifference except that she wasn't indifferent—she couldn't be.

The twins were already inside, standing perfectly still and awe-struck on the shining parquet floor of the hall, looking with wide eyes at the curved staircase with its wrought-iron banister, turning slowly round to look at each door that led off from the hall. They had never been in any house like this before, and when she had first come here neither had Carrie.

Coming from a cottage in the country, she had never quite lost the feeling, when she had lived here with Matt, that she was living in a palace. The twins were clearly a little overwhelmed. In Sydney they had lived in a flat, and the fact that it had been a very nice one did nothing to prepare them for this house.

'Miss Caroline!' The twins actually jumped as the

door at the end of the hall opened and Ruby erupted into the hall. She was just the same, a thin vigorous woman in her sixties, her iron-grey hair short and straight, her face showing a severity that had frightened Carrie until she realised that it was a feature over which Ruby had no control, she just looked like that, it had nothing whatever to do with the way she felt.

The twins watched her nervously, Gemma stepping slightly behind her sister, as Ruby bore down on them all, her arms already open to receive Carrie.

'There! We've got you home at last and looking just the same!' Her great motherly hug left Carrie breathless and smiling and she turned on the twins at once like a determined whirlwind. 'And Mr Silver's little lambs! Alike as two peas in a pod! Well I never! Let's see what we've got in the kitchen. I made a batch of toffee specially when I knew you were coming.'

She had them under her spell at once with these well-chosen words and Gemma relaxed noticeably, allowing Ruby to take her hand and lead her off with Pippa to the kitchen.

'That child is going to be as fat as butter,' Matt murmured in astonishment, his mind obviously going over the quantity of lunch that Gemma had consumed not more than an hour ago.

'She worries it all off daily,' Carrie said absently. Her mind was still reeling from Ruby's greeting of the twins, as 'Mr Silver's little lambs'. He had meant, then, every word he had said, and she knew without being told that everyone at the wedding would have been quietly given the same information. He had claimed the twins openly and she was back at Falconridge. The file could be closed and anyone who had ever looked at Matt with pity when he and Carrie had gone their separate ways would now understand that it had been an unfortunate temporary separation. She wondered what her long illness was supposed to have been. He had probably told people that she had gone stark raving mad. She wouldn't put anything past him. Matt was not a loser, he never had been and he had the patience to wait for whatever he wanted. Everyone was now slotted neatly into place, a little extra room made in the file for the twins.

'You'd better come along and see what you think of their room,' Matt said quietly, bringing her back to the immediate present. 'I'll get the cases in a minute but you can inspect their room while they are otherwise occupied.'

It was on the tip of her tongue to thank him sarcastically for allowing her to have anything to do with her own children but she thought better of it before she had spoken. It was as well to move very carefully with Matt. He had told her so very clearly that he was not in any way indulgent now and she supposed that she should be thankful that he was actually, apparently, very indulgent with the twins.

The room was towards the back of the house, a pretty room with twin beds and white furniture obviously prepared especially for them, and she wondered how he had ever managed to get it all fixed up in time. He seemed to be reading her thoughts because he stood by the door watching her and said softly, 'People are remarkably willing to act fast if you wave enough money under their noses, and I wanted the girls to have a place that would be their own particularly. I wanted them to have it right from the word go.'

'You've certainly moved fast since Wednesday morning,' she muttered, looking round at the new decoration, the new curtains.

'Not quite as fast as that,' he said comfortably. 'I had every intention of marrying you and brnging the three of you here from the moment we talked at the dinner that Carter-Rousseau gave.'

'But you didn't know I'd agree!' She spun round

and looked at him with a quick feeling of alarm.

'I knew you were no longer married,' he corrected. 'That's all I needed to know. Getting you to agree was relatively easy. I never doubted that you'd be here eventually. All I'd ever needed to do was to find you, and that was not in any way by luck. Normally I don't need luck. After that, it was simple. I was prepared to go to any lengths.'

'You went to sufficient lengths, I think!' Carrie said bitterly. 'You threatened to ruin Allan!'

'Merely the first line of attack,' he assured her smoothly. 'I always have back-up plans.' His wry amusement left her wondering what his other plans would have been if this one had failed and he straightened up and looked at her intently as her eyes showed a quick burst of fear.

'You're afraid, Caroline?'

'No. I know you well enough to know that you mean what you say. The file is closed. We can all get on with our lives now as best we can.'

'As best we can? A strange choice of words,' he murmured coming slowly closer. 'And what makes you think that the file is closed, I wonder? To my mind there are quite a few odds and ends that have to be sorted out before that happens. People,' he stressed sardonically, 'now know where Carrie is. People will be relatively satisfied when all this wonder has died down and they have something to think about that doesn't concern us, but I'm not in any way satisfied.' He was closer to her than she had realised and he suddenly grasped her shoulders and pulled her hard against him, looking down at her with hard eyes.

'You vanished, Caroline. I went away for a few days only, days that unfortunately stretched into a longer time than I had intended. When I came back, the house was empty, Ruby in tears, the little shy bird had flown, now you see her, now you don't! And you were nowhere to be found, you seemed to have stepped off the world.'

He cupped her face in hard hands, hurting her in his intensity, frightening her with a kind of deep, boiling violence that was only just beneath the surface.

'Where the hell is Carrie?' he said with quiet viciousness. 'Is she alive? Can she cope without me? Has she had an accident, lost her memory, been kidnapped, murdered? But you coped well enough, didn't you, my sly little babe with violet eyes? You were off into another bed, into other arms while I was going quietly mad. No, Caroline, the file is not closed, the debt is by no means cancelled!'

'I—I didn't think that you'd look for me.' She could hardly speak because of the tight pressure on her face but she managed to get the words out somehow, the wrong words because his grip seemed to tighten even more, his stare to become more punishing.

'I bet you didn't! But I looked for you, Caroline! Like a fool! I was convinced that you had simply gone out and something was preventing you from coming back. I even thought of going to the police to report you missing. What a fool I'd have looked then! But I remembered about Jenny, Jenny who spent so much time in Wolverhampton. I went round to that dismal bedsit and she told me. Carrie had left the country, gone to Brazil as an au pair, gone off with an English family and Carrie didn't ever want to see me again!'

'You believed her?'

'Oh, I had no choice, did I? She showed me the postcard you'd sent just before you got on the plane. I remember every word. "Thanks for everything. Don't worry about me. I'm really happy and looking forward to a new life." You wrote that, Caroline! You were the one who was really happy!'

She remembered the card. She'd posted it just before she and Allan had boarded the plane for Sydney, a dismal thank-you note—something she had been brought up to believe was an essential of good manners, and Jenny had used it to silence Matt.

'I went to Australia with Allan.'

'Yes, I found that out. After a while I stopped feeling stunned, stopped feeling anything but a cold rage. Then, I really started to look for you! I traced the loving cousin easily enough and I got the news back from Australia that there was no Caroline Stuart, but a girl with the same face was very efficiently running the Sydney office—a Mrs Haley! Such good fortune! I had expected to have to drag your address in Brazil from Croft and there you were, right in the bag! It took me three years to get a big enough interest in Carter-Rousseau to wield power, but it was the biggest interest of my life for those years, especially when I realised that you'd gone straight into the arms of Mr Haley, straight into Mr Haley's bed!'

She wanted to scream at him that it wasn't true, to tell him about the twins, but her hurt went too deep. For all she knew, he had every intention of going back to Florida whenever the mood took him. He had married her for revenge and to set the record straight and she was going to have to pay and pay. Kevin Haley had been a protective armour around her for over four years and he was still her only protection.

'How can such innocence hide such sly treachery? You really fooled me. You really took me for a ride with your wide violet eyes and your strict grandma. Even when I saw you the other week, looking so defenceless and beautiful at that dinner, for a second I almost fell for it again, until I remembered that ring on your finger, those little girls!'

'You can hate me as much as you like! I don't care any more! Do you understand? I've got the twins to remind me of happiness and I've got nothing else. There's nothing, absolutely nothing you can do to make me more miserable!' She wrenched her face away from his cruel grip, staring at him white-face, her voice rising.

'No, I can see that.' Some of the towering rage seemed to have left him as soon as she spoke of the twins, at the very mention of them his expression softened.

'Where's my room?' she demanded shakily, wanting to lock herself away although she knew it wasn't possible. Gemma and Pippa would be coming up at any moment and she had to get control of herself.

'Along the passage,' he said quietly. 'Opposite my room, our old room. You can hear the river from there too and it's got the same view, more or less. The guest-room we never allowed guests to use. Do you remember, Carrie? It would have meant them being too close to us and we never wanted anyone close to us, we only wanted each other. Do you remember?'

'Stop it! Stop it!' She put her hands over her ears, refusing to listen to the voice that was suddenly quiet, deep and warm, like the Matt she remembered but he pulled her hands away, holding her wrists.

'Why? Does it hurt? It hurt me for a long time. It's your turn now, Carrie.'

And suddenly she couldn't bear it any longer, she tore her hands free and ran blindly from the room, along the well-known passage, slamming the bedroom door behind her and bursting into tears.

He was there almost as soon as she was, opening the door and grasping her shoulder, spinning her towards him.

'Wrong room, Carrie,' he informed her softly. 'This is our old room and I sleep here alone now, unless you've really come home.'

She looked round wildly and he was right. Instinct, habit, whatever it had been, she had run to security and there had never been any of that, except with Matt.

She couldn't halt the tears to order and they just

kept flowing as he cupped her face, wiping them away with his thumbs, gently.

'Have you come home, Carrie?'

'No! I don't know what you're talking about,' she sobbed. 'Let me go!'

'Oh, I'll never let you go, Carrie, not again. I thought you understood that. This time it's for good. But you've forgotten what home is like, I think. It's been over four years. I'll remind you.'

She struggled but it was useless. She was still a mere slip of a girl beside Matt's strength and height and he held her with ease, grasping her short curls, forcing her to meet the hard pressure of his lips.

Her frantic movements were only wasted energy and she was too tense, too overwhelmed by the past that whispered to her like so many small phantoms in this room to keep up any fight.

At the first sign of her submission, the hard grip of his arms relaxed and his kiss softened to a gentle exploration of her mouth, softened almost to tenderness until time slipped completely away and she was young again, in love, back at Falconridge and in Matt's welcoming arms. Her eyes closed and her arms found their way around his neck as she sank into the bliss that had been the past.

She didn't even know when he stopped kissing her and only opened her eyes when she heard the sound of his voice. She was stunned, bewildered, her tears miraculously ended as he looked down at her, his hand still cradling her head.

'Home is like that, Carrie,' he said deeply and quietly, 'and I think you've missed it. I think that in spite of Mr Haley you've been very homesick.'

She came to her senses and pulled free as she saw the glitter of amusement in his eyes, the cruel twist to his mouth.

'Don't flatter yourself! I was too busy being happy with Kevin, too busy rearing the children to give one thought to anything else. Is the experiment over? Or was that a part of the continuing punishment to set the record straight?'

'If you like.' He leaned against the door and simply looked at her coolly.

'Then let me know when I've paid off all my debts, will you? But do try to think up some other form of punishment, that form is a little too barbaric.'

'I'll see what I can do,' he promised coldly. 'Meanwhile, I'll bring up the suitcases.' He turned to leave but looked back over his shoulder, his eyes sardonic. 'Maybe I'd better remind you that you're trespassing. This is my room, Caroline.'

'Get a notice made! Private! Keep Out!'

'Is it going to be necessary, then?' he enquired softly, walking out as her pale face flushed deeply.

CHAPTER FIVE

CARRIE almost ran across the passage into the room that was ready for her and stopped inside the door feeling stricken and lost. The little treasures that she had abandoned when she left were all there. Her books, the little fat ceramic dog that Matt had brought home after she had seen it in a shop window and stopped to laugh at it. The porcelain clock with the golden numbers, the white cane chair that didn't really fit in anywhere but which had been delivered the day after she had admired it.

She was still standing stunned when Matt came back, putting the cases inside her room.

'You'll have to sort out which case is which for yourself,' he said, the episode of a few minutes ago apparently forgotten. 'And the twins are about to arrive. Better pull yourself together.'

'I am pulled together!' she snapped, turning to glare at him, but he simply shrugged lazily.

'Just advice,' he murmured with a reasonable air that infuriated her. 'Don't smash up your treasures. If you don't want them we'll give them to a jumble sale.'

The twins came racing along the passage, obviously already happy in the house, and she went quickly to the mirror to check her appearance, startled to find that she looked perfectly normal.

'We've lost Mummy,' Pippa giggled, knowing perfectly well that it wasn't true and therefore treating it as a lark. 'She's disappeared.'

'Yes, she does that. I've noticed it myself,' Matt

said infuriatingly. 'Come and look at your room, it's along here.'

'I'll show them!' Carrie stepped into the passage, her voice sharp and Matt's lips twisted into a mocking smile.

'We'll show them together, shall we?' he murmured. 'You've developed a tendency to turn in the wrong direction since we've come into the house. Let's play for safety.'

She never answered but her tightened lips seemed to give him a great deal of satisfaction.

The twins loved the room and instantly began to plan exactly where they would put their things.

'Speaking of their things,' Matt said quietly,' where are they? Surely they have more possessions than you could cram into these suitcases?'

'They're in Sydney,' she said tightly. 'They're crated. Now that we're—settled, I'll send for them to be put on a boat.'

'Give me the address where they are and the necessary papers and I'll arrange for them to be flown out,' Matt offered immediately.

'But you can't!'

'Why can I not?' Matt looked at her sharply, obviously annoyed, and she felt utterly at a loss.

'The cost! They can easily come by sea.'

'The cost?' He looked at her scathingly. 'What does cost matter to me? Their toys are important to them. We'll get it all arranged later.'

She wasn't sure if she welcomed his possessive attitude towards the girls or if she was suspicious of it. He had already got them eating out of his hand, so to speak, and his eyes rested on them now with warmth and pleasure. She felt a tingle of unease at the way he had taken to two children whom he thought belonged to another man and, knowing his way of thinking nowadays, she couldn't be sure that he wasn't playing some devious game to punish her through the children. It made her want to shut him out, to keep them close to her as the only happiness she had.

'Let's get your clothes,' she said firmly. 'Then you can wear your jeans until bedtime.'

Their moans of protest, their pleas to be allowed to explore the house first, had Matt turning to them severely.

'Mummy knows best,' he said with finality as he left the room. 'For now,' he added quietly for Carrie's ears alone, and she knew he had some plan that she wasn't going to like at all.

She took them later to explore the house and Matt was nowhere to be seen. She knew the old house so well, and as she wandered from room to room, its atmosphere gradually got a grip on her. All the remembered, well-loved things were here and the white baby grand in the wide window of the drawing-room drew her like a magnet. She had delighted Matt when he realised that she could play well and she sat down now and played for the girls who curled on the settee to listen, surprised that there were things about Mummy that they had never known.

Gradually her skill came back and she was lost in the melodies that floated out and filled the room. She was back in the past, to the time when she had first come to Falconridge, Matt readily commuting to the city because he wanted her to live in the country air.

While they occupied the flat, she had continued at college, finishing the term, but Matt had never liked it. He was restless and irritated when she was out of his sight, waiting for her every day, long before her last lecture was over, pacing up and down beside his car and only relaxing when he saw her.

But she blossomed under his possessiveness, feeling completely safe instead of crushed, and she willingly abandoned her course at Redland when they moved into the country. They both wanted a home and Falconridge became that.

If she had imagined that he would hide her away, she could not have been more wrong. Wherever he went she was beside him, at dinners, parties, visiting friends, until her confidence grew and she slowly changed into 'that beautiful young woman with Matt Silver'.

As she blossomed, other people began to pay attention to her, especially men. At first, Carrie was too wrapped up in Matt even to notice, but Matt noticed. The first time she had been puzzled and uneasy to find the honey-brown eyes turning to icy gold, but later she was left in no doubt. She had been to a party with him and she had been dancing with a young man only a couple of years older than herself, oddly enough, a Yorkshireman. They were deep in conversation as they danced, reminiscing about places they both knew, like two aliens who had met on a strange planet, when Carrie was suddenly wrenched from his arms by a savagely angry Matt.

He offered no explanation, he simply held her tightly, dancing silently with her, avoiding her hurt and questioning gaze.

'Matt?' She found the courage to speak after a few minutes but his grip only tightened and his answer was a low growl of anger.

'Not now!'

She bit her lip and look down. For the first time, they were quarrelling and she had no idea why. Tears began and she couldn't prevent them from coursing down her face and he noticed, pulling her head to his chest, obviously sorry.

'Let's get the hell out of here!' he muttered, swinging her to the door, leaving without a backward glance, his arm tightly around her.

In the darkness of the car he pulled her roughly

into his arms, not really soothing her but with an air almost of desperation.

'I don't want you getting friendly with any men at all!' he stated with frightening intensity, 'You're mine!'

'I love you, Matt!' She was shocked and hurt. He looked at her for a long time and then gathered her to him with a sigh.

'Do you, Carrie? Is there enough love to last?' he asked quietly. As usual when they returned to Falcon-ridge she was drowned in the sweetness of his lovemaking, secure again, but the incident clouded her mind for days.

Ruby accepted her from the first; to her she was Miss Caroline, Mr Silver's lady, and life took on a peace and beauty that would never end. Except that it did. It ended on the morning that she received a letter from Allan, reading it eagerly, not realising that Matt too had received a letter that was absorbing him.

They had turned to each other, both speaking at once but Matt had never heard her news, had never known that Allan had the contract in Australia and was going there at once without even the time to call on her. Jenny had forwarded his letter and Carrie knew that he would be in Australia even now. Matt's own letter was too much on his mind for him to show the usual interest in hers.

'I'm going to America,' he said abruptly and her heart sank. He didn't say that she was going with him, and that in itself was unusual. Everything she had heard from Vivienne rushed back into her mind and her face was pale and distressed, but he was too deep in thought to notice, his words to her almost vague.

'I don't know how long I'll be but you'll be all right here. Ruby is here and you can use the other car if you want to go anywhere.' He peeled off a thick wad of notes and put them into her hand. 'This should last you until I get back but if you need anything else, ring John Carmichael.'

The speed of his departure left her feeling breathless and forlorn as if he had suddenly forgotton about her altogether. In fact for a few seconds she thought that he was not even going to kiss her goodbye, although he did, deeply suddenly sweeping her up into his arms and holding her tightly to him, an odd look on his face that she failed to understand.

He left within hours of the letter's arrival and for the rest of the day she was lonely and lost, wandering around miserably until Ruby suggested that she should find herself something to do, turn out a few drawers, polish the piano, anything, because Ruby complained that she was making her miserable too.

So Carrie started with the bedroom, turning things on to the bed and putting them back methodically into the drawers, knowing that it didn't really need doing and feeling no less unhappy, but not as unhappy as she felt when she came across the letter.

It was right there in one of Matt's drawers, staring up at her and she had no chance of not seeing it and getting the gist of it, although she didn't take it out. The writing was heavy, black and clearly visible, and the words seemed to spell the end of her life.

'I should have phoned but it's not my style. You had my letter, Matt, and you know how things stand. I want you to come back so that we can sort things out between us. I don't want any anger now. Come as fast as you can.'

It was signed Yvette and there was a photograph too, though whether that had come with the letter, Carrie didn't know. All she did know was that Matt had kept it, a photograph of a very beautiful woman, delicate faced, soft-eyed and lovely, the same black writing scrawled across the front: 'To my dearest Matt. In case you've forgotten.'

For ages she sat and stared at that photograph, at

the lovely, sophisticated face, feeling that Yvette was everthing that she herself could never be. She looked at the words of love written across the bottom of it and her heart slowly broke into little pieces. Yvette had called and Matt had gone instantly because she wanted him back. Carrie wanted him back but she knew that he would never come. She would get a letter or a phone call, regret in his deep warm voice, an explanation of Yvette and their need to be together, and she couldn't face waiting for that.

Almost in a daze she gathered her things, walking out of Falconridge without any plans or ideas as to where she was going, her leaving so silent and lonely that Ruby had never even seen her go.

She had walked to the road and had just kept on going, carrying her suitcase, never even feeling the weight, and she was on the train to London before she came to herself, before she realised that she had nowhere to go. The cottage was sold, her only money her small share in its sale because she had left the notes that Matt had pushed into her hands on the bed after she had tidied up the room. Allan was so far away and she knew no one else. And then she remembered Jenny and that was where she went, to stay in the bedsit and refuse to go out, almost cowering from the hurt.

It was there too that she had discovered that she was pregnant and had sworn Jenny to secrecy about Matt. Even when Jenny had searched Carrie's bag and found Allan's address in Australia, even when he came and swept her out of the despair into a new life, they had both refused to disclose the name he demanded to hear, Jenny because of her promise and Carrie because she loved Matt and would never stop loving him.

She was startled and embarrassed suddenly to find that both Matt and Ruby were standing in the doorway listening to her playing. Her eyes had been staring at the wall, her thoughts over four years away, and she suddenly found herself looking into Matt's eyes.

'Lovely, Miss Caroline,' Ruby said in a croaky voice, her eyes a little damp. 'That last one was so sad but it was always my favourite. The piano's never been touched since you left . . . I mean . . . '

She glanced anxiously at Matt but he wasn't listening, he was just staring at Carrie bitterly, the little warmth he had shown recently completely gone.

'I'll get it tuned,' he said abruptly and walked out. It somehow made her feel like an intruder, as if she had calmly walked into somebody's house and had begun to play their piano without permission, because Matt went to his study and never came out even at dinner time. The children had been given an early meal and had been put to bed and so Carrie ate alone, feeling cold, wretched and unwelcome.

Matt went out early the next day, and as it was Saturday she knew it was unlikely that he would be visiting his office, and indeed he had not because he was beck at lunchtime, carrying a huge box which he placed before the two excited girls.

'Open it,' he invited as they circled it anxiously. They pounced on the box and began to unfasten it with more eagerness than skill.

It required Matt's help and Carrie was left with the forlorn feeling that it had little to do with her. The gasps of the twins were almost echoed by Carrie as the box revealed two beautiful identical dolls, such cxquisitc crcaturcs, so large, so beautifully dressed that Carrie wouldn't have dared even to look at the price in a shop window.

'Mummy!' Gemma's little face was a picture of delight and Carrie found herself swallowing hard to control tears.

'They're—they're beautiful,' she managed. 'They're going to need names, I expect.'

It was a flash of inspiration of her own that had

them making rapidly for the stairs to discuss the necessary naming in the privacy of their room.

'Er——?' Matt's voice stopped them and they came giggling back to say thank you and Carrie didn't know whether to be glad or jealous when their thanks ended with the word 'Daddy' and when they flung their arms around his as he crouched down by the box.

They fled, and so did Carrie, walking quickly into the drawing-room to stare out at the cold, overcast day.

'All right! What did I do wrong? Where have I sinned?' Matt's voice with an edge of anger came from the doorway and she didn't turn.

'You haven't done anything wrong. The dolls are beautiful and the girls love them.'

'But you would rather that I hadn't bought them?'

'I've no idea why you should get that impression . . . ' she began but he interrupted harshly.

'Your lack of enthusiasm spoke volumes.' He paused and then added, 'You imagine that I'm trying to buy their affection? I expect that's just the kind of thought that would slide into your devious little mind.'

'It's not in my mind!' She turned on him bitterly. 'It was never in my mind for a second! If you must know, I was upset because I've never been able to afford to buy them anything like that. Those dolls are a little girl's dream. I couldn't have even glanced at the price in the window.'

'So, Haley had little to offer except his wonderful character?' he queried sarcastically. 'Well, you can buy whatever you like now both for the twins and for yourself and I can't see why the dolls should grieve you or make you feel inadequate. They've clearly managed well, even without a father. You've given them years of love and it shows on their faces. There's no doll that can compensate for that.'

'There was Allan,' she said quietly.

'Yes, I begin to see that he has more going for him than an ugly temper. Perhaps, after all, he's going to be worth my effort. Let's get this straight though, the dolls are a gift, not a bribe!'

'I never imagined otherwise,' she said wearily. 'You were always generous, Matt.'

He was against her in two strides, furious instead of being placated.

'Generous! You thought that's what it was, as if you were some kind of casual mistress? I worshipped you! I was terrified when you were out of my sight because you were too wonderful to be real! I never wanted to see the smile leave your face. I was so much in love with you that I couldn't believe such happiness could last! Well, it didn't!'

He was staring at her with a look akin to hatred and she couldn't even begin to answer. His constant bouts of bitter anger bewildered her and left her totally dazed. Yvette might never have existed. She would never confront him with it, whatever he said. She would never let him see the depths of her hurt, but she knew that Yvette existed and still existed. It seemed that she must shoulder all the blame and be berated for the rest of her life for marrying a non-existent man. She dared not think of her vulnerability if he should ever discover that Kevin Haley was a myth and the girls his own.

Her silence seemed only to have embittered him further, and he turned away.

'There's no point in all this, is there? I didn't marry you to roar at you day in and day out. Nowadays you bring out every bit of savagery that's deep inside me. Just stay on the very edge of my life, Carrie, and we'll try not to irritate each other too much.'

He strode out but came back almost at once, his face cold. 'I quite forgot,' he said tersely. 'As you're my wife I suppose you're entitled to know where I am when I disappear from time to time. I'll be going to a dinner tonight and there's no need for you to accompany me, it's strictly an all-male affair.' She merely nodded uninterestedly and he strode out again with a quick mutter of exasperation.

She dined alone for the second night and Ruby's pursed lips said all to clearly that she sensed the atmosphere and liked it not at all.

'Time was when Mr Silver wouldn't have left you alone,' she observed as she cleared the table.

'It's a men-only, Ruby. I'd look pretty stupid there.'

'Time was when he'd have refused to go, then!' Ruby rejoined grimly. 'I'm not going to see you get all poorly again!'

'You mustn't interfere, Ruby,' Carrie said anxiously, but Ruby merely sniffed.

'I've got my methods,' she asserted airily. 'I've known Mr Silver since he was a boy, Mr Matthew he was to me then, before he went off to Cambridge and then to America without coming home. It took him long enough to search for me when he finally got settled in England again and I can leave just like anybody else. I'll remind him how he was when you walked off like that, too poorly to know what you were doing.'

'Please don't, Ruby!' She almost asked Ruby to tell her what disease had been diagnosed but she was really too busy trying to placate the irate housekeeper.

'We'll see!' Ruby said darkly.' I'll put those two lambs to bed now.'

'I'll do that!' They had been left to play longer tonight with the new dolls and as Carrie had had an earlier than usual meal, they were not too disastrously late.

'You settle to rest,' Ruby ordered. 'You're pale as a little ghost. All that lovely colour you used to have gone. You should never had been allowed to get a tan when you were away, it only fades and leaves you sallow.'

She swept out, leaving Carrie feeling more super-
fluous by the minute, recovering from an illness that
nobody would tell her about and obviously looking
fairly pathetic with a skin like a faded leaf. She found
herself smiling, amusement rising over misery as she
went off to bed to reread one of her favourite books.

It was eleven o'clock when Gemma came in to
enquire pitously if there was anything to eat. Apparently she had played off her supper and hunger had
awakened her.

'You can have a drink of milk and a biscuit,' Carrie
promised, getting into her dressing-gown, her eyes on
the slender child who could eat anything put before
her. Maybe now that she was settled she would become
more confident and the alarming habit would fade.

'Get back into bed, darling, I'll bring it up.'

She was filling a glass with milk when Matt came
back, coming straight through into the kitchen.

'Oh! It's you.' He stopped in the doorway and then
came slowly in loosening his tie. 'You're hungry?'

'No, it's Gemma.'

'That figures. She's not the only one, though, I'm
starving.'

'Are you?' She was almost holding her breath. They
were speaking normally like two people who knew
each other well. For the moment there was no hatred
and she hardly dared continue.' What did you have
to eat at the dinner?'

'Nothing, wonderfully cooked and graciously
served,' he observed wryly. 'You've been to these
affairs. How many times have we come home and
cooked ourselves something substantial afterwards?'
He suddenly seemed to realise how he was speaking
and looked away abruptly. 'Want to make me a ham
sandwich?' he enquired huskily.

'Er—yes, yes, of course. I'll just take this to Gemma.'

'I'll do that.' He had the glass out of her hand

before she could protest. 'I might eat the biscuit myself on the way up.'

She stood in a daze for a second after he had left and then hurriedly got out the bread, butter and ham. He seemed to be ages because the sandwiches were ready and she had cleared up before he came back.

'Was Pippa awake?' she asked without looking round.

'No, Gemma and I whispered. It seems that Pippa is giving serious consideration to calling her doll Ruby. Gemma's doubtful about the wisdom of that. I found myself in agreement.'

Again the smile was hovering on the edge of Carrie's lips and Matt looked at her steadily for a second.

'You want to share these?' he enquired, indicating the sandwiches.

'No! No, I'll go, unless you want me to make you a drink?' He simply shook his head, watching her until she left hastily, feeling that she ought to be backing out of the kitchen to keep her eyes on him as long as possible. There had been a growing warmth in him that she wanted to cling to and he looked as he had looked when she had first seen him, tall, powerful, handsome and unknowingly protective.

The little feeling of happiness made her restless and she couldn't get back into bed. She found herself pottering about the room doing absolutely nothing and she was just telling herself firmly to get into bed when Matt tapped on the door.

'I forgot to tell you something,' he said quietly when she called for him to come in. 'I'll be working from home for a while. It's going to be difficult enough for your cousin to work with me, without the interested eyes of a full office staff looking at him every time he comes in. Also, I expect he'll want to raise his voice from time to time and the study's reasonably soundproof.' He paused and looked at her ruefully when she didn't reply, simply standing there in her pink dressing-gown, her hands in the pockets, watching him seriously. 'You know, he does need help, Carrie,' he continued quietly. 'The firm would have eventually folded in spite of his brilliance, somebody else would have had the benefit of all his ideas. He's got to learn to delegate responsibility for one thing. He'd have been far better off, too, just closing the Sydney office and moving for a while to where the job happened to be as it needed his expertise.'

'He wouldn't let me live out there after . . . ' She had been going to say after the twins were born but she shied away from it. Any mention of their birth might give him a clue and he was quick to see anything. Her unfortunate trail into silence however brought a quick frown to his face because obviously he had thought that she meant after Kevin Haley's supposed disappearance.

'Be that as it may,' he said tightly, 'he's got to reorganise his thinking unless he wants to be in the position of being merely a working inventor. Brilliant he may be, but businessman he is not. However,' he continued before she had the chance to say anything, 'the point is, we'll work from here and I've taken on a temporary secretary. Barton's too valuable to leave the main office.'

'Barton?' Carrie stared at him, not really interested in who Barton was but glad that the burst of irritation seemed to have passed.

'Barton,' he repeated, 'my secretary.' She showed interest then and astonishment.

'That's what you call her? Barton? Not Miss Barton or Mrs Barton?' Matt looked surprised, straightening up from the door, his dinner jacket slung over his shoulder.

'I don't know whether she's a Miss or a Mrs. I've never noticed. I'm not sure if she's anything, except damned efficient. She likes being called Barton, it's her own idea.' He paused and then added wryly,' She doesn't exactly please the eye.'

'You should have kept Rosemary!' He'd probably like to have a pretty secretary prancing around the office, she thought, and with the thought came a great burst of jealousy that sharpened her voice.

'Kept her?' Matt looked surprised both by her remarks and by the acid tones she used. 'As I remember, Rosemary called me a pig!'

She just couldn't imagine it and burst into laughter, covering her mouth with her hand, another habit from the past that he noticed and his eyes widened and warmed instantly.

'So, then, you fired her?' She tried to control her laughter but it was really hard, Rosemary had been a calm, smiling woman.

'Hell, no! She said it as she handed in her resignation. She told me that I'd reverted to type without you and she couldn't face going back to that. Obviously I'd been a pig previously. I'd really no idea!'

She couldn't stop laughing and her attempts to keep her voice low so as not to disturb the twins, turned her merriment into a fit of giggles that had Matt closing the door. He slung his coat down and moved across to her, his eyes smiling.

'Will you stop giggling? You're as bad as the twins! I'd no idea that they'd inherited that infuriating habit from you. I thought they must have picked it up from Haley. I'm bitterly disappointed. I'd planned to have weeks of enjoyment imagining him giggling.'

But she couldn't stop even when he grasped her shoulders and then, unexpectedly, her laughter turned to tears.

'Carrie! Don't!' He pulled her into his arms and for a second held her tightly. 'I'm sorry, I shouldn't have said that. It was unfair and bitter. I honestly didn't mean to make you cry.'

'It's not—it's not . . . ' She wanted to tell him that

it wasn't because he had mentioned Haley at all, in fact she had no idea why she was crying, except that she was permanently tense nowadays, always on edge, on guard, when before she had been so happy and relaxed with Matt.

'It's not what?' He suddenly let her go, angry and cold again. 'Not possible to forget him? I really don't care one way or the other! If you want to walk hand in hand with a ghost, then just keep doing it!'

He had everything wrong, it seemed that everything she would do for the rest of her life would be misinterpreted and raged at and the brief moment of happiness had been wiped out by the cold look on his face that was clearly always going to be there.

Misery and frustration boiled over inside her and she flew at him, sobbing and angry, beating her clenched fists against his chest, too distraught to come out with any words.

For a second he was startled and grasped her wrists, stopping the furious onslaught. Then he looked at her with narrowed, thoughtful eyes as she struggled and sobbed in his grasp.

'I wonder why you're really crying?' he murmured quietly, 'I wonder where all this frustrated desire to attack me is coming from. Do you want to be back in my bed, Carrie? Do you?'

The deep quiet of his voice shocked her into immobility and she was still staring at him with wide, frightened eyes as his lips closed over hers.

Instantly she struggled, determined not to fall back into the past as she had done upon her arrival in this house but he simply tightened his arms, grasping her curls and tilting her head back until she was powerless to move at all. And then his lips plundered hers with an angry determination, not seeking any response but forcing one. With an almost cruel pleasure he drove her back from the edge of reality that she tried to cling to in her mind until her stiff and resisting body softened and she sighed against his hard lips and surrendered.

He grasped her face, waiting until she opened her eyes to meet the fury and bitterness in his.

'Who's winning this battle?' he asked savagely.' Don't think that I'm going to step back into your sly little world, that I'm going to forget your treachery just because I remember your body!' He stared at her with angry resentment, as if she was the one who had instigated this and she realised that he was fighting a battle inside himself, that he too remembered the past, but it did nothing to ease her own ache.

'Damn you, Carrie! I want you! I never could keep away from you. I hate you but I want you back in my arms, back in my bed!'

He pulled her tightly against him and it seemed that he was just letting a frightening passion run amok. He had never made love to her like this before. He had always been gentle, loving, but now there was nothing but a soaring sexual desire and the lips on hers were hot and devouring, the hands that roughly pulled away her dressing-gown and tossed it aside were on the edge of brutality.

But she was starving for him, over four years without his strong hands on her skin, his body against hers. Memories flooded over her, nights of bliss, days of happiness and her little cry of longing brought a blaze of tawny fire into his eyes.

There were no thoughts in her, no realisation of the future, only memories of the past as she felt the heat of his lips through the thin silk of her nightdress as he hungrily sought her breast. His hands on her hips were like steel, hurting, but she hardly felt it.

'Come to my bed, to our bed,' he demanded urgently. 'I want you back there just like it was before. I want those arms around me in the moonlight, your skin against mine. I want to own you again!'

She had almost fallen completely into the dark

depths of his desire but his harsh demand to step completely into the past brought her back to the present. She wanted to go, she was desperate to, but what was left of the past? Her life would always be one of bitterness, Matt's eyes accusing her every day. He wanted to own her again as he had before when she had imagined it was love. She had been an obsessional interest to be cast aside when the woman he loved wanted him back. Now she was a wife who was to be for ever punished. To sleep in his arms again would rob her of every bit of self-respect, would crush her finally.

'No!' She tried to pull free but he grasped her tightly. 'No! I'll not let you spoil something beautiful. I'll not face second best. I'd rather be alone for ever, just remembering!'

All the passion died from his face, leaving him cold and hard at once, his skin pale and his hands fell to his sides.

'So live with your ghost then!' he bit out harshly. 'He must be some great hero to keep this hold on you when he's dead. I couldn't keep a hold on you so I'll give him best. We'll live our lives as best we can, as you said so pertinently!'

He strode from the room, picking up his jacket and closing the door with a quiet finality that said more than any angry words.

CHAPTER SIX

BREAKFAST next morning was an ordeal and would have been worse had it not been for the chattering presence of the twins. Without being obvious about it, Matt was not speaking to her and this morning he even seemed disposed to ignore Gema and Pippa, although they were still too excited about the new dolls to notice.

Ruby walked into the unhappy silence that stretched like a cord of pain between Carrie and Matt to announce a visitor.

'A Miss Trevere!' she informed Matt, her eyebrows raised in very clear disapproval but Matt merely nodded and left the table without a glance at Carrie. She heard voices in the hall almost at once.

It couldn't be the same person, she thought frantically, it couldn't be the polished, scheming Vivienne, but she knew deep down that it was and when the door opened again, she knew really what to expect.

'Caroline!' Vivienne Trevere's face was a mixture of shock, disappointment and genuine surprise as she stared at Carrie.

'My wife, Miss Trevere,' Matt said coldly. 'As you'll be here for some time, you'd better meet everyone. The twins are Gemma and Pippa, our daughters.'

If she hadn't been feeling so stricken, Carrie would have laughed. The disappointment on Vivienne's face was now pitiful. Working with Matt at last only to discover a cosy little family. She could almost hear Vivienne's thoughts.

Her own thoughts, however, were not disappointed

102

ones, they were miserable and frightened. Just the sight of Vivienne threw her headlong into the past, into her first shy glimpse of Matt. Everything that had happened rushed through her mind and she could see him looking at her at that awful dinner, his eyes meeting hers across the room. She could see him with the white roses and the way he had treated her in a fatherly manner, biding his time. She could hear his voice when he had asked her to come with him, to live with him and be his love and she remembered that first night in the flat, the first time ever that . . .

He was watching her intently, coldly, as if she were part of an interesting experiment, and she knew without doubt that Vivienne's arrival was no accident. He had chosen his temporary secretary with care. The maximum punishment with the minimum effort and it must have been planned for days, he had only bothered to tell her last night.

'Hello, Vivienne, it's very nice to see you again.' She hated to mouth platitudes, to hear them rolling uneasily off her tongue, and it wasn't nice to see her, it was frightening. She didn't want Matt to be with anyone else; jealousy was like a knife inside her. 'So you finished the course?'

'Finally,' Vivienne laughed, her eyes on the glitter of Carrie's rings, the broad golden band of her wedding ring and the hoop of flashing diamonds that Matt had placed on her finger immediately afterwards. 'You didn't, though! We all wondered where you'd disappeared to.'

'She was otherwise engaged,' Matt interrupted stiffly, clearly not liking the trend of the conversation, causing Vivienne to turn slightly pink and look at him from the corners of her well made-up eyes. It gave Carrie some small amount of satisfaction. He probably did not know that Vivienne had a disconcerting habit of trilling out any thought that flitted through her head. 'If you've finished your reunion, darling, I'll take Miss

Trevere and get her acquainted with the necessary work.'

The derisive voice was aimed at Carrie, but Vivienne clearly no longer felt like a visitor. His tone had dismissed her from the privacy of the room and his family.

Carrie sat on at the table after the girls had scampered off with Ruby and her thoughts swung from annoyance to jealousy and back again. She had never tried to be glossy. She had attained a beauty that was deep and lasting but she was as unaware of it as if she were still nineteen. She felt drab beside such a butterfly and finally she went to seek out the telephone directory, choosing a hairdresser almost at random by the largest advertisement in the yellow pages. It was time to empty the ever-full pot.

She marched into the study later, already dressed to go out, never knocking, her eyes as cold as Matt's.

'I'm going out, darling,' she informed him, using the same bitter tones that he had used earlier. 'Which car can I take?' He stared at her for a second and then stood slowly, his eyes never leaving hers, Vivienne glancing from one to the other with deepening interest.

'You can take the Mercedes, it's easy to handle. I'll get it out for you.'

'There's no need. Just carry on,' she invite him blithely.

'I'll get it out!' He took her arm and almost hustled her from the room, closing the door, crossing the hall and shutting them both into the privacy of the dining room.

'Where are you going?' he demanded harshly, swinging her to face him.

'I'm going to London to do some shopping.' She had expected indifference, to see Vivienne's shapely legs swinging almost under his nose but there really had been work going on in there, work that he had now abandoned.

'You're taking the girls?'

'No, Ruby can take care of them. I'll be quite a long time.'

'I'll drive you there and wait for you.'

'No!' He was beginning to annoy her, she didn't want anyone to come and spoil her plans. 'I'll be ages and I don't want anyone with me.'

'Why?' There was so much annoyance in him that she felt sure he was going to refuse to let her leave the house. 'You're meeting someone?' he asked with aggressive intensity.

Her temper flared then. Meeting someone! Who, for heaven's sake? Except for Alan there was no one in the world she cared about or even knew other than the people in this house who were her whole life. Even Jenny had left London!

'Will you stop jerking me about!' she demanded angrily. 'If I can't have the car, I'll call a taxi and spend even more money. As you seem to be so ferociously interested in my movements, I'll tell you! I'm going to have my hair done and I'm going to spend as much money as I can in one day!'

His grip relaxed and he looked at her with none of the aggression he had shown seconds before, but there was a vibrant look about him that she didn't much care for.

'Spend away,' he invited softly, 'I doubt if you can empty the bank in one day.' His eyes swept over her golden curls. 'What do you imagine anyone can do with that hair except cut it shorter? Even in the rain it curls more.'

'I'm having it straightened!' she snapped untruthfully and spitefully and he grabbed her hard, glaring at her.

'You wouldn't dare!'

'It's my hair. I'll do whatever I like!'

'You are merely part of a bargain,' he informed her nastily. 'Remember? Lock, stock and barrel? I count

the hair an asset and therefore it is not to be altered.
There were no negotiable terms in the contract!'

She wasn't sure if he was really serious in this
astonishing assertion or if he was laughing to himself,
certainly there was a gleam in his eyes and she snapped
out in exasperation, 'Oh, give me the keys and get
back in to your glamorous secretary!'

'I'll get the car out,' he said softly, taking her arm
in a reasonable manner, his grip only tightening when
she attempted to pull away.

'Take care,' he cautioned later as she took the keys
and prepared to drive off after he had manoeuvred
the long car out on to the drive. 'Remember that
you've never driven this before, it's got a lot of power
under the bonnet.'

'I've got a lot of sense under my bonnet,' she
snapped. 'I'm not a fool.'

She started the engine but he leaned in at the open
window.

'Carrie,' he said quietly and when she turned to
look at him angrily he continued, 'if you try to
disappear, I'll find you.'

'You've got hostages!' she reminded him bitterly.

'Even if I hadn't, I'd find you.'

'You'd really bother?' she enquired scathingly and
he gripped her face hard.

'I'd make if my life's work! To the ends of the
earth, Carrie!' His mouth came down, crushing her
startled lips in a long, punishing kiss that left her
weak and shaken, and then he was striding back into
the house, leaving her to sort out the car and to give
thanks that it was automatic—her legs were weak.

It was miles before she recovered and she didn't
want to think about Matt's threat or what it meant.
Every day he would think up something, she was sure.
No doubt they would have Vivienne as part of the
family for as long as it amused him, because certainly
he wouldn't expect her to drive to and fro every day,

it was much too far. She could foresee the time too
when Ruby would hand in her notice and stalk off
from Falconridge if the atmosphere continued, and
that thought was most unwelcome. She would have to
do something about it before it reached crisis level.

Once in London, though, she cast her worries, her
jealousies and her fears aside and set out to do
something she had never done deliberately in her life,
to spend money and enjoy herself.

It was very late in the afternoon before she turned
the car once again for home.

Matt was nowhere to be seen when she arrived and
she staggered up to her room with her boxes and
parcels, kicking off her shoes tiredly and wondering if
it had been worth the effort. But it had, she decided
as she looked in the mirror. She had had her face
professionally made up, her hair was swept to one
side glamorously and she looked older, more sure of
herself, sophisticated.

She went in to see the twins as they were being
prepared for bed and they were satisfactorily
enthusiastic, comparing her with their glamorous dolls,
to which comparison Ruby merely muttered. 'That's
it all right,' and made no further comment, her severe
face this time mirroring her severe thoughts.

But Carrie was not crushed. A long look in the
mirror as she prepared to go downstairs revealed her
new self, her smoothly glamorous face, her sophisticated hairdo the perfect foil for the deep blue dress
she had chosen for this evening, one of her expensive
purchases.

She had never thought before of anything so daring
and the cleavage gave her momentary doubts as she
looked at herself, admitting that it left little to the
imagination. She was not given to wearing slinky
creations and this dress was definitely that but she
lifted her head proudly and went down to dinner. No

doubt Vivienne would be there and if she had to slink
then she would do it well.

They were in the drawing-room with cocktails and
she made an entrance that stunned them. Vivienne,
seemingly jaded after a day's work, looked decidedly
peeved and Matt just stood staring, his eyes sweeping
over her so many times that she felt dizzy.

'You're safely back, darling, I see,' he got out at
last. 'I thought I heard the car ages ago.'

'I've been to see the girls and Ruby,' she informed
him easily. 'Oh, pour me a cocktail, darling.' She was
charming, brittle, just like the women at the affairs he
attended in the line of business and he actually blinked
in surprise, knowing full well that she hated cocktails
before dinner.

'Miss Trevere will be staying at Falconridge for a
while,' he said quietly as he turned to get her drink
but Carrie was ready for the little trick.

'Oh, good! I was going to suggest it myself. It's too
far to' travel each day. Why, it really will be fun
having company each day, Matt.'

She walked forward to collect her drink and his
eyes followed her every movement as he withheld the
glass until she was close enough to touch. He didn't
touch her, though. Instead, his eyes roamed over her
hair, her face and then deliberately lingered on the
barely concealed rise of her breasts.

'Company will make a nice change for a while,' he
agreed softly, his eyes never leaving their inspection
of her until she felt her cheeks flush. 'But Miss Trevere
will really be terribly busy, darling. I expect she'll be
almost too tired by dinner-time to exchange reminis-
cences with you.'

'Oh, Vivienne, have you had a hard day?' She
turned her back on Matt to escape his eyes but that
was a big mistake. His hand came to her shoulder and
then to the back of her neck, massaging her nape
softly, his fingers wandering on to tease her spine in

the old, remembered way and there wasn't a thing she could do about it. He knew how she was feeling, how this had always made her feel. It was all she could do not to melt back against him and he was totally ignoring Vivienne's embarrassment.

'I'll just nip up to my room for a handkerchief,' Vivienne blurted out desperately and fled, her departure a signal for Matt to pull Carrie back against him, his arms around her waist.

'*Touché*—darling?' he murmured derisively in her ear.

'Let me go!' It was hard to put up any kind of a struggle and she realised belatedly that he had never even bothered to hand her the cocktail she had asked for so unnecessarily.

'If you set out to excite me surely you can't be surprised when I get excited?' he asked in an amused voice, his lips beginning to blow softly against her ear.

'I didn't!' she gasped, still trapped against him but he laughed quietly.

'Let's pray you never do then. I'd have a heart attack.'

His hands wandered up to cup her breasts and then she really struggled, while she still could, springing away from him and feeling decidedly unsophisticated when he merely picked up his drink and watched her with a long look of golden-eyed amusement.

'You're—you're . . . !'

'Completely in control,' he finished for her with nasty sarcasm. 'How do you feel, Carrie?'

Vivienne's return saved her and they dined in an atmosphere that clearly made Vivienne wish that she was motoring back through the dark, because although Matt did nothing to offend, his eyes were constantly on Carrie, teasing her throughout the meal until she felt ridiculous and childish. But Vivienne was obviously getting other vibes, and Matt was doing it with a deliberate determination to bring Carrie to the unsure state she had been in at the beginning of the day.

She was thankful to get to her room after dinner and the dress was in the wardrobe on a hanger, her dressing-gown on—but only just—when Matt simply opened the door and walked into the room.

'Out!' She glared at him and his eyebrows rose mockingly. 'What do you want? You've no right to simply walk into my room!'

'This is my house, you are my wife and therefore it seems to me that my rights are paramount,' he corrected coolly.' The time will come, I think, when I'll simply take anything I want and consider the consequences later.' She blushed deeply and he simply stood looking at her, his face still, frightening her with his power deliberately until her legs were trembling. 'However,' he added, when he could see that he had subdued her in the quickest way possible, 'I really came this time to see if the glamour washed off or if it's permanently sprayed on. I'm a bit too soon, though, I see, you haven't let it approach water yet. Perhaps you're thinking of sleeping with your head on a wooden block all night, like Japanese ladies of old?'

He was making her feel as painted as a geisha and she raged at him in a small fury.

'Why are you being so unspeakable rude?' It was difficult to keep her voice down and she didn't want him to shut the door, not after his opening announcement, but he merely raised his eyebrows and shrugged lazily.

'It's my nature.'

'It's not! You're deliberately trying to make me feel stupid and—and painted!'

'You are painted,' he assured her, his eyes drifting over her with growing annoyance. 'I told you a long time ago what would happen if you tried for that look. The bargain was Croft Computers saved in exchanged for Caroline Stuart, as normal, as seen previously. I will not vary the terms!'

'Stop talking about me as if I was a—a commodity!' she snapped.

'You are a commodity,' he snapped back, 'and that's all you are. Today you've deliberately and childishly damaged the product. Get it restored to normality by morning or I'll do it myself!'

He turned to leave and her anger bubbled over as she raised her voice.

'You can just go and . . . !' She never finished, but he looked back at her with sinister intent.

'I also require the girl with the standards laid down by Grandma,' he rasped. 'We all know that it was a pretence but I prefer to go on pretending and what I prefer is the thing that will happen. Appear like that in the morning, Caroline, and I'll leave Miss Trevere to get on while I give you a good hot shower. Who knows,' he added quietly, 'anything may come of that.'

Any desire to fume died quickly as her heart began to race with fear and an uncomfortable burst of excitement that showed on her face before she could run away. He raised one speculative eyebrow.

'Just let me know when the heat gets too much for you,' he said quietly before closing the door and leaving her to herself.

In the morning, it was all more than she could manage anyhow and she went down to breakfast looking only like herself, with a head of crisp shining curls and delicately applied make-up. Not that Matt seemed to notice. He did not speak to her, but Vivienne had apparently recovered from her embarrassment and seemed to have assumed that Matt's behaviour of the night before was normal, that this was some kind of love nest. And Carrie felt pleased to see her after all because Matt read his mail, answered the twins' little remarks briefly and then left without a word.

Vivienne seemed captivated by the girls and lingered to talk to them until Matt's rather irritated, 'Miss

Trevere?' from the doorway had her finishing her coffee hurriedly and leaving quickly.

And Carrie soon found out why he was so irritated. Allan arrived, ushered in by Ruby, her face relaxing into a smile as Carrie leapt up and the twins rushed to him shouting, 'Uncle Allan! Uncle Allan!' at the top of their voices.

'How are things?' he enquired quietly, giving Carrie a hug when he had been introduced to Ruby, smothered by kisses from the twins. They were alone as the girls raced off to fetch the new dolls to show him.

'Fine, Everything's fine,' she assured him but he looked at her quizzically.

'There's a typical Carrie remark if ever I heard one. Well, you're still in one piece anyway, and I'll be here regularly for a few days. I can't think why we're working here but I'm glad. It means that I'll be able to see you and the girls and watch the progress of this odd marriage closely.'

Before he could say anything else, Matt appeared almost at the same time as the twins, Vivienne trailing along behind him with a notepad as if she were expected to take down every word he uttered.

'Daddy brought us these, Uncle Allan!' Pippa announced stridently before anyone else could speak, and Allan's eyes flew to Carrie, his expression startled. She managed to shake her head to indicate that she had not told Matt about the girls, her face feeling hot as she realised that Matt had missed nothing of this brief exchange.

'When you're ready, we'll begin,' he announced stiffly, eyeing Allan with little enthusiasm.' Unless you'd like coffee first?'

'Later, thank you,' Allan replied in an equally unbending voice and, rather desperately, Carrie brought Vivienne into the circle.

'My cousin Allan, Vivienne,' she said quickly.

'Allan Croft of Croft Computers,' Matt added

coldly, clearly intending to take any warmth out of
the situation and clearly intending to keep Vivienne in
her role of secretary and nothing more. He failed
dismally though. Vivienne was not the norm in secretaries and she drifted forward with plenty of
confidence, her eyes on Allan with growing interest.

'Oh! Croft Computers. We've been going through
your affairs yesterday, in fact we're well on now.
They're not nearly as bad as I thought. Daddy was
sure the firm would fold, he's a broker, you know,
and he's not often wrong, but I can see he's wrong
this time. We'll see what we can do.'

It was difficult to say who was the more enraged,
Matt or Allan, but Allan got his fury out first.

'Who the hell is this bouncy female?' he demanded
violently, his eyes on Carrie after one searing glance
at Matt.

His unaccustomed rudeness left Carrie actually open-
mouthed and even Matt was stunned into silence.
Vivienne, however, was not in the least perturbed.

'Vivienne Trevere,' she laughed, grasping his hand
and shaking it vigorously before he could prevent her,
leaving Allan stunned in his turn. 'Now, don't confuse
enthusiasm with interference, Mr Croft. I've had quite
a few ideas myself over yesterday. If you'd like to
come into the study I can show you what Mr Silver
has worked out so far and I might say too . . . ' She
walked off briskly, clearly expecting that he would
follow, and he did, looking thunderous.

'I take it that she's not a private secretary,' he
observed sarcastically to Matt, 'as she seems to think
that my affairs are a free-for-all. Did you invite
"Daddy" down too to offer advice or do you intend
to lock her up until the work is over? I'd better see
exactly what she knows about my affairs before I
strangle her!'

He strode off and Pippa's plaintive 'Uncle Allan!'

only received a terse 'Later', as he deliberately slammed the breakfast-room door.

Carrie looked at Matt expecting to see rage, instead his eyes met hers with wry acceptance of the situation.

'The irresistible force and the immovable object, something's got to give,' he said ruefully. 'Maybe I deserve this. God give me strength!'

His own progress to the door was halted by Pippa, determined to have a word with somebody.

'Did you send for our toys from Australia, Daddy?' she asked, looking up into his face.

'I did, Pippa. I sent for them straight away.' His hand came to stroke her head. 'I'll tell you as soon as they arrive and if they're delayed in London, we'll drive up and fetch them.'

'And I will?' asked Gemma quickly.

'And you will, my little mouse,' he assured her, tweaking her nose and going off to join Allan leaving them both giggling once again.

Expecting to hear sounds of violence from the study, Carrie thought it a good idea to take the twins out and presently, in jeans and fur-lined parkas, their feet in warm boots, the three of them were walking in the park towards the river. In spite of her warm clothes, Carrie found herself shivering frequently, but the twins declared themselves to be as warm as toast so she stayed out, her pleasure somewhat marred by a few irritating little bouts of coughing but her eyes feasting on the scene she had never forgotten.

The river was high and threatening and she didn't walk too close with the twins but they could all hear the constant sound of rushing water. Even in the pale, fitful sunshine, though, the grass wet beneath their feet, the trees dark and outlined in stark beauty against a troubled sky, the twins were so clearly happy that Carrie felt her own spirits lift.

Nowadays their excited chatter was peppered with frequent references to Daddy where before the only man in their lives had been Allan. Matt's behaviour towards them still astonished her. She had been speaking only the truth the other day when she had said that he had always been generous, but to take to another man's children so soon with so much affection was stretching generosity to its very limits and she sometimes longed to tell him that he really was their father. Only her fear kept her silent, fear that he would at some time go off to Florida again and leave her to wait in obedient despair. Her hurt was still too deep to ignore that possibility.

Another fit of coughing had her turn to the house again after a while and when they got back, it was to find the others having a coffee break.

'Are you all right, Carrie?' Allan was on his feet the minute he saw her and his concern seemed to irritate Matt at once. 'You've got two patches of high colour. You're not feeling ill, are you?'

'Of course not,' she said brightly, realising as she said it that she wasn't feeling any too well and hadn't been for a couple of days. 'It's the wind. It's really cold. We came in earlier than I intended because of that.'

'Personally, I avoid weather of all kinds,' Vivienne informed them, her shapely legs crossed at the knee.

'I can imagine!' Allan cut in sarcastically, his eyes sweeping over this hot-house flower. 'You arrived here wrapped in cotton wool and carefully packed, I assume?'

To Carrie's surprise, Vivienne had no reply. Instead she flushed and looked quite hurt, and Allan muttered under his breath while Carrie hastily ushered the girls out to the hall where they were instantly captured by Ruby. Matt followed, climbing the stairs behind her and sauntering into her bedroom uninvited.

'Perhaps you should get that Keep Out sign for my room,' she said sharply as he came further in.

'I'm seeking sanctuary,' he confessed with unexpected frankness. 'I've got myself into a situation bristling with danger. I can't cope with Cousin Allan and Miss Trevere in the same room together. I never trained to be a referee.'

'It serves you right,' she said with a certain amount of malicious pleasure. 'It's hardly Allan's fault that you chose a butterfly with a loudspeaker as a temporary secretary. Obviously you like the glossy type so you'll have to make the best of it or return her to wherever she shimmered out from yesterday.'

'I didn't choose her for her gloss,' he said quietly, clearly deciding to ignore her tone. 'Having, as she informed me, taken the Redland course three times, she's absolutely astonishing with shorthand and typing. I've never seen such speed, but I hired her because she used to be a friend of yours. I thought perhaps you needed some company. You seemed pretty wan and lost.'

'I have company!' she rejoined bitterly, hurt beyond words to feel that her thoughts when she had met him—that he imagined that she was like Vivienne, out to capture a wealthy husband—had been correct after all. 'I have two daughters and I get on famously with Ruby. Furthermore, Vivienne Trevere was never at any time a friend. She was hardly even an acquaintance.'

'I thought you'd be reasonably pleased to have someone you knew to talk to,' he said quietly, any friendliness dying out of his face. 'I see that I wasn't included in your list of company, not that I expected it.'

'Nor do you want it! I know my place as a commodity, thank you. To be presented as originally viewed, wrapping to remain intact.'

'Except that it didn't, did it?' he retorted with equal bitterness. 'The product was handled by Mr Haley.'

'Oh, just go away and leave me in whatever peace I can gather around me!' Her face felt flushed, she was hot and the dry tickling in her throat brought tears to her eyes as she went into a hard fit of coughing.

Matt walked out and she sat on the bed, racked with the dry cough, unable to stop. She still hadn't stopped when he came back, a spoon and bottle of syrup in his hand.

'Come on, take a couple of spoonfuls of this magic elixir,' he ordered. 'Ruby swears by it.'

'I'm all right.' His return had surprised her and she found herself pulled to her feet as he poured the mixture into the spoon.

'Open wide.' He was treating her like a child and she obeyed without thinking, glad of the soothing mixture as it trickled down her throat.

'It's good stuff, this,' he asserted, putting the spoon and bottle on the dressing-table. 'Ruby used to force it on me when I was a mere youth. I got to like it. I may take it up again and give up whisky.'

She couldn't imagine why he was being so nice suddenly and she didn't want to look at him in case she found that his eyes were hard again as usual. 'You spilled it on my parka,' she said quietly, glad of the excuse to look down and away from him.

'I'm sure it will sponge off. Anyway, it's too hot to wear a parka indoors. No wonder you look so flushed.'

Before she could act, he had unzipped her jacket and as she raised startled questioning eyes, he slid his hands inside, pulling her towards him.

'If we're going to fight regularly, I want it to be hand-to-hand combat,' he said sensuously, his hands finding their way under her sweater. 'I enjoy fighting at close quarters so much more, and you've acquired an alarming ability to come out equal first in a stand-off fight.'

He looked down at her and she could only stare helplessly into the honey-brown eyes, not understanding their sudden tenderness at all, looking frightened and wary. She needed him with a deep and

desolate longing that found its way on to her face.
She stayed quiet in his arms, all her fight gone.

'I expect it's the motherly instinct that finally sharpened your tongue,' he murmured, watching her, 'a
she-cat with her kittens.'

'Allan did all my fighting for me,' she managed to
whisper, not wanting to say anything at all, just to go
on looking at him.

'Yes, you're very close. I can see that. He clearly
knows so many things that I don't know. If he wasn't
your cousin, I could get very angry at the little looks
that slide between you.'

She stiffened, then understanding the reason for this
subtle attack. He had noticed Allan's startled look
when Pippa had called Matt Daddy. He was letting
her know, reducing her first to this foolish submission.

She tried to pull free but he simply pulled her close,
his hands warm and persuasive on the skin of her
back, his head bending until his lips were brushing
her neck. She gave a trembling sigh as his hands slid
to span her slender waist and move upwards to allow
his thumbs to tease her aroused breasts.

'Want me, Carrie?' he whispered against her lips as
she shuddered with a burst of wild feeling.

'No! No, I don't, I . . . '

'Say yes, Carrie,' he murmured, his mouth brushing
hers. 'You want me and I want you.' His mouth
stroked her gently, slowly and insistently; his hands
stroked her with the same drowsy rhythm until she
wanted to forget everything, but she could not. Kevin
Haley was a lie, with no substance, no reality. She
had never even imagined a face for him, he had been
a name to hide behind and nothing more. But Yvette
was real, her beautiful, delicate face still in Carrie's
mind as if it had been only yesterday when she had
seen the photograph. Yvette was part of Matt's past,
part of his future, and she would never go, just as

Matt would never cease to punish her for leaving without his permission.

She gave a little cry of pain and as her lips opened he claimed them, his mouth opening over hers, his hands instantly possessive, moving over her warm back, urging her closer until they were locked together, their bodies moving in unison, seeking each other with growing desire.

'Sooner or later, you'll come to me,' he murmured against her lips. 'If there were not hordes of people in the house, you'd come to me now. You're lonely for the room across the passage.'

'I'm not!' she managed to get out, trying to fight the feelings that were drowning her but she got no further.

'Yes, you are,' he said with harsh certainty, his fingers impatient on the waist band of her jeans. 'It may spoil your beautiful memories of Haley that you're so anxious to cling to but right now you'd be happy to be in my arms, in my bed, and don't imagine that the heat will lessen. It's going to grow.'

She had no time to react to the fear that flooded over her. He had her trapped, and his statement when she had agreed to the marriage that she would sleep alone with her beautiful memories was so clearly a part of the punishment. What would he do? Reject her at the last minute? As her body began to stiffen and grow icy cold, Ruby's voice from the doorway penetrated the clouds where she had been for a few blissful seconds.

'Well, what was it all about, then?'

'What was what about?' Matt enquired vaguely, his eyes, still on Carrie's face, narrowed with a growing triumph.

'The cough mixture! I saw you get it while I was seeing to the girls. Who's coughing?'

'Carrie was,' Matt said, still holding her close and disregarding Ruby's presence. 'It seems to have stopped now but I'm really beginning to think that she's not too well.'

'I'll see to her!' Ruby bustled in, not one bit embarrassed, looking ready to pull Carrie out of Matt's arms if necessary.

'I might say, Mr Silver, that there's raised voices in your study and with the twins around I don't really think . . . '

'Neither do I,' Matt agreed, releasing Carrie after one deep and unfathomable look into her hurt eyes. 'I had hoped that they'd reach deadlock but it seems that I'm going to have to wield some authority.' He moved to the door and Ruby didn't wait for him to go.

'Now then, Miss Caroline, you're not going to get any better until you're in bed,' she said firmly, like Nanny.

'I said that not more than a few seconds ago!' Matt observed with a sly astonishment. 'You've got second sight, Ruby, unless you were listening round the corner.'

'Get along with you, Mr Matthew!' Ruby retorted, red-faced, quite forgetting her present position. 'You always were too forward!'

His narrowed eyes mocked Carrie as he left but she was too busy trying to argue her way out of being put firmly to bed to give him more than a blushing glance. In the end, she argued herself into the lead and got away with two aspirins and the cough mixture and a promise to remain indoors.

Ruby had lit a fire in the drawing-room and Carrie played there with the twins as a dull afternoon followed a troubled lunchtime and the day darkened with approaching rain.

She was glad that Matt was fully occupied, she hardly dared to think about him. It was clear what part of her continued punishment was to be and she really had no idea if he truly wanted her or not. For

all she knew, he could be simply pretending a desire.
Her knowledge of men and love was confined solely
to Matt and he had never been like this before.
Memories of how he had been in the past when he
had seen her, how his arms had opened for her eager
love, how he had been so adoring, so tender were now
so little use to her in face of his stated desire.

CHAPTER SEVEN

THE girls were allowed to play for a while in the gardens immediately near the house, but Carrie was kept strictly indoors by an ever-watchful Ruby who darted from window to window, following the progess of Gemma and Pippa like a faithful sheepdog with its flock of sheep.

They were all taking tea in the drawing-room later, the atmosphere just a little improved from lunchtime, when the storm broke. Driving rain lashed against the windows of the old house with such ferocity that they all looked around, startled. The wind had risen steadily during the late afternoon and now it seemed to be a screaming fury behind the rain.

'Is this going to frighten Gemma and Pippa?' Matt asked quietly, but Carrie shook her head.

'No, they'll love it. Ruby will just have difficulty keeping them at the table long enough for them to finish their meal.'

Giving the girls their last meal of the day was a task that Ruby had taken over with a steely-eyed determination. They ate in the kitchen as she prepared dinner, the constant chatter of the three of them telling all too clearly the good relationship already established between the stern-faced woman and the two little girls.

Matt nodded, satisfied, and she caught Allan's look of surprise, a surprise that settled into thoughtfulness. The battle between Allan and Vivienne seemed to have reached a state of truce and Carrie imagined that to be the result of Matt's intervention. At any rate, they were civil to each other and Vivienne didn't look quite as huffy as she had done earlier.

'I'd better get these curtains drawn, Miss Caroline,' Ruby stated, bustling in and stepping across to the tall windows that overlooked the garden. 'There's nothing to see out there anyway, it's black as pitch.' Her task completed, she looked around the room in surprise. 'I'd better feed those two hungry terrors too. I thought they were here.'

'They were coming to you when the rain started,' Carrie said, jumping up. 'They'll be upstairs, I'll get them.'

She was out of the room before anyone realised it, her panic-stricken face hidden. They were good little girls, always doing exactly as they were told, and if they had decided to go upstairs instead of going to Ruby, they would have come to tell her. Gemma in any case would never be late for one of Ruby's special suppers.

Their room was empty and so were all the other bedrooms and Carrie raced downstairs to find Ruby standing puzzled and slightly worried in the hall. Obviously she had searched down here and found nothing. She looked at Carrie anxiously and shook her head but Carrie simply rushed past her, opening the front door and racing out into the gale-force wind and the torrents of rain, never thinking about the blackness, shouting their names in a wild panic, the river on her mind, as Ruby screeched, 'Miss Caroline!' in a loud frightened voice.

Carrie was almost blown over, groping around the side of the house, drenched to the skin in seconds by the icy cold rain, her only hope the constant calling of their names. There were so many corners to turn, so many things to trip her, but her heart leapt with relief as she rounded the side of the house and found them crouched by the side of the wall close together, too small and frightened to turn into the force of the wind.

She just fell on her knees in front of them in the mud, her arms hugging them close, sobbing her relief and happiness and then two powerful arms grasped her and she was pulled to her feet as Matt towered over them, his strength like a miracle.

'Hold me tight!' he yelled, picking up the twins and they did, clinging to his neck with all their might, leaving him free to put one sheltering arm around Carrie, 'Come on!' He turned into the wind and driving rain, half dragging Carrie when she stumbled. The light from the open door had never seemed more welcome.

'Get back!' he ordered sharply as both Allan and Vivienne were preparing to dash outside and join the search. 'There's a limit to how many wet people one household can cope with.'

'Thank goodness!' Ruby rushed forward to take the two bedraggled and scared children. 'You were that quick, Mr Matthew! You left us all standing.'

'Get them dried and fed, Ruby, and into a warm bed,' he said shortly, his eyes on Carrie. 'I don't suppose they'll be any the worse for wear but I'm not sure about Carrie.' She was shivering uncontrollably and he marched her to the stairs.

'Can I help?' Vivienne's voice never stopped his momentum.

'Yes, shut the door, for God's sake, and then see if Ruby needs any assistance.'

'Daddy!' Pippa's little wail stopped him and he turned quickly 'It's Betty! She's all wet! We went to get her because I forgot to bring her in.' She burst into tears holding up the doll that she had determinedly clutched and brought back to the house. It was ruined and Carrie sniffed unhappily at the sight of Pippa's distress.

'It will be all right,' Matt said distractedly. 'Just let

Ruby see to you and then we'll get around to Betty's problem.'

'She's all spoiled,' Gemma said in sympathy and burst into tears too.

'No, she'll be fine,' Matt was torn between the twins' misery and Carrie's nonstop shivering. 'Look, Ruby's going to sit up all night with Betty and get her well. Ruby used to be a nurse.'

'That's right. Bring her along,' Ruby said after a surprised look at Matt as she took in this startling information. 'She'll probably be as good as new in the morning,' she added with a threatening look at Matt as she hurried the twins upstairs to the main bathroom, Vivienne in tow holding a dripping doll and looking at Matt with amazement. Matt Silver had never given her the impression that he could behave like this.

'Now you!' Matt said briskly as he half pushed, half lifted Carrie upstairs. He was soaking wet himself but he took her right through into her own bathroom and turned on the hot shower.

'Under that smartly,' he ordered. 'I'll get changed and be right back.'

She was so cold, shivering so much that her hands could hardly cope with her wet clothes and in the end she just stepped into the shower as she was, peeling off her clothes as the water warmed her hands. She felt so ill that drying herself was an ordeal that took all her strength and when Matt came back she was sitting on the edge of the bath in her dressing-gown, her hair dripping wet, sobbing away as much as the twins.

He had changed into grey slacks and a dark red sweater and she raised tear-drenched eyes at his startled exclamation.

'You—you look nice,' she sobbed as he came purposefully forward, picking up a towel *en route,* his eyes on her hair.

'Thank you. That remark proves that you're delirious. It's bed for you and no arguments. Why, for heaven's sake, didn't you tell me what you were going to do? You're in no state to face a gale. You should have been in bed for the past two days by the look of you.'

He began to towel her hair vigorously but she had a fearful headache and her tearful protests stopped him. It didn't stop him from sitting her on the dressing-stool and wielding the hairdryer though with no thought for anything but getting her warm and into bed.

'You've made me look like a poodle!' she sobbed as he ran his hand through the curls and declared them to be dry, and with a little smile he lifted her into his arms, hugging her close when she clung to him and put her wet face against the strong column of his neck.

'Come on,' he said softly. 'Into bed. You'll be really sorry about all this delightful submission tomorrow. It's sure to bring on a bad attack of waspishness.'

There was a knock on the door and when Matt called out, Allan came in, a little startled to see Carrie in Matt's arms, her own arms round his neck.

'I wondered if Carrie was all right,' he began uncomfortably and Matt looked at him for one long serious moment and then moved to the bed.

'I really think that she's got 'flu, but tomorrow will tell. Wait for me a minute, will you? I want a good long word with you.' He popped Carrie into bed still in her dressing-gown, drew the blankets over her and walked out with a very puzzled-looking Allan.

It was a good while before he came back and he looked very satisfied with himself.

'One more disturbance and then you get dinner in bed,' he promised, sitting her up.

'What's that?' she asked warily, her eyes on the voluminous garment in his hands,

'One of Ruby's nighties. I know yours, there's nothing to them. This is the old Victorian variety. I can hardly wait to see you in it. You'll look just like Gemma.'

Her protests had him looking at her quietly, his eyes warm.

'Stop it,' he ordered softly. 'I know every inch of you and you're not well enough to be at risk from me.'

'What about Betty?' she asked when she was safely back under the bedclothes, feeling warm and comfortable in the thick, old-fashioned cotton nightie.

'Betty is a write-off,' he said ruefully.' Or to be more precise, a wash-out. However, Allan has just gone and in the morning he'll arrive with an exact duplicate. Thereafter, a little trickery and we'll be restored to peace and tranquillity.'

'It took you a long time to tell him that.' He was calling Allan by his name, behaving as if there had never been any sort of trouble between them, and she wondered uneasily what the long talk had been about.

'You were impatient to get me back?' he enquired sardonically, seeming to relent immediately as her face showed signs of distress. 'We had a sort of cousin-in-law chat,' he added in a more kindly tone and stood looking at her in silence for a minute. 'I'll get get your dinner sent up. Ruby is furious with me for appointing her Nurse of the Year, I have to dine alone with Miss Trevere, God's in His Heaven, all's right with the world.'

He turned and walked to the door but her voice stopped him.

'Why—why are you being so nice, Matt?' She had to know what was going on in his mind. Since she had been out in the storm there had been a very subtle change in the atmosphere and she felt uneasy about it.

'Well,' he leaned back against the closed door and

watched her with unreadable eyes. 'I went to a great deal of trouble to recapture you. I have to protect my property, don't I? If you were to die of pneumonia, think of the monetary loss!'

She looked down, hiding her eyes and the swift rise of blinding pain that had swept across her at his words and when she looked up he had come back very quietly to stand by the bed.

'Or, there again,' he added with a deep sort of weariness, 'maybe I've got too much memory of the past to see you in any way ill or distressed. I always thought that I was protecting you, caring for you, old habits die hard. You say that I took the stars from your eyes, well, maybe I did. God, I'm getting so that I don't know any more!' He stood looking down into her eyes for a second and then his lips tightened and he walked to the door. 'I'll send up your meal,' he said abruptly, walking out and she hoped that her feelings had not been showing on her face. She loved him so totally, so completely that without him, life had been a cold, empty thing, in spite of the twins.

Next morning there was no doubt in anyone's mind that Carrie had influenza, least of all in her own. Well dosed with aspirin and a hot drink by an unusually harassed Ruby, she had slept deeply, only waking with the occasional fit of coughing, which had invariably brought Matt into the room. By morning she had gained the hazy impression that he had been up all night.

She slept late and was finally wakened by the whispering of the twins as they stood rather anxiously in the bedroom doorway.

'That's far enough in,' Matt ordered quickly when, seeing her eyes open, they would have rushed in to her. 'We don't want anyone to get Mummy's germs, do we?'

They looked doubtful but obeyed, and then both began to speak at once.

'She's better! She's better before you, Mummy!'

'Look at Betty! She's all right again!'

The doll in question was in splendid form and clearly brand new.

'Oh, what a good nurse Ruby is!' Carrie croaked painfully. 'I'd no idea that she was so good.'

'It's all the years of training,' Ruby said tartly, coming up behind the girls and cunningly beginning to lure them away with promises of elevenses.

It seemed to be visiting time because Allan appeared too, grinning at Carrie and making her feel like Rip Van Winkle because there was such a change in the general atmosphere that she felt she must have been asleep for months.

'Betty's dress is cleaner than my Sue's now,' Gemma said thoughtfully. 'She looks more new.'

Ruby's eyes flashed in panic to Matt and even Allan, the great story-teller, looked to Matt for inspiration.

'Her dress was beautifully washed and ironed,' Matt explained seriously, adding craftily, 'if you'll just hand Sue over to Ruby for the whole day, I expect she'll do the same thing for her. It does take a whole day though.'

'It's all right,' Gemma said quickly. 'I like Sue as she is. It's all right, thank you.'

'Sensible girl,' Ruby applauded, looking at Matt as if she were ready to spank him. 'I can put my laundry-maid's diploma back in the drawer with my nursing certificate then, can I, Mr Silver?'

'I should think so,' Matt said smoothly, and she stamped off with the girls.

'Can we see them?' Pippa begged as they went.

'One of these days,' Ruby promised darkly.

Allan was having a hard time to stifle his laughter and Carrie felt that everything was going just a little over her head.

'Very cunning,' he granted, looking admiringly at

Matt. 'Decidedly Machiavellian!'

'Spur of the moment,' Matt assured him airily. 'Given time, I can come up with really good ideas.'

Just for a moment, Allan's face darkened and Carrrie thought it was a good time to intervene.

'You must have come early,' she said as best she could with her painful throat.

'Only twenty minutes ago,' Allan said, looking at his watch. 'Betty was confined to sick bay until I arrived. We did the switch a few minutes ago and then you had to be told. How are you, Carrie, love?'

'Definitely not "just fine", anyway,' Carrie smiled.

'I'll order you something to eat,' Matt said briskly, 'and then we'll get on, Allan. Miss Trevere is already at work.'

'Oh, lord! For one blissful moment she'd slipped my mind!' Allan groaned, following Matt from the room. 'See you later, love,' he called to Carrie, and Matt didn't seem to mind at all.

'It was all too puzzling for somebody with a throbbing headache, she decided, as she went on wobbly legs to the bathroom for a quick wash and to survey her tousled image in the mirror.

She was just trying to brush some order into her hair with hands that could hardly hold the brush when Matt reappeared with a breakfast tray and lifted her without a word back into bed.

'This,' he said crisply, 'you will undoubtedly recognise as a bed! See to it that you stay here until I give you permission to get up.'

She nodded, feeling too dizzy to argue, only too glad to be back. He stood over her while she picked at her food with little interest, tucking her up carefully when she finally pushed the tray away.

'Stay put!' he ordered, and when she simply looked up forlornly into his face, he muttered angrily under his breath and suddenly bent to place a hard, fast kiss on her lips.

'You'll get my germs,' she said unsteadily as his eyes moved over her feverish face.

'I've just got to watch that I don't get more than that,' he murmured with evident self-disgust, his golden eyes gleaming. 'A germ goes in a few days. What I got before took longer.' She had to close her eyes to shut in the tears but he knew they were there. 'Go back to sleep, Carrie,' he said with a deep quiet, his hand on her curls, 'Just forget that I spoke.'

It was much later when the sounds of banging and the odd shout wakened her. She was feeling much better, though still a trifle dizzy, but the sounds were so alarming that she hurriedly got out of bed and staggered to the door in her long, thick nightie The sight that met her eyes left her stunned.

Allan, Vivienne and Matt, all in gum boots, were at the top of the stairs, Matt and Allan carrying the long settee from the drawing-room and Vivienne looking absolutely astonishing in one of her beautiful, slim-fitting, exotic dresses, gum boots at least two sizes too big neatly touching the hem.

'Carrie!' Allan's sharp call had Matt spinning round and dropping his end of the settee as he leapt towards Carrie who stood swaying dizzily in the doorway, utterly puzzled by the unexpected sight that had met her eyes.

'For God's sake, Matt!' Allan roared, staggering under the sudden weight, nearly overbalancing and definitely not helped as Vivienne clutched him anxiously. 'Will you let go, woman?' be bellowed. 'Matt's just done his best to knock me downstairs. He doesn't need any help!'

'I was only trying to save you!' Vivienne yelled back and then burst into tears.

'Oh, lord! I'm sorry. There now!' In front of Carrie's astonished eyes, Allan put an arm round Vivienne and that was all she saw. Matt swung her up and kicking off his gum boots, carried her determinedly back to bed.

'You,' he said earnestly, 'are a troublemaker.'

'I only came to see what it was all about, all that uproar,' she protested weakly, definitely dazed by the events.

'You appeared in that nightie like Lady Macbeth and nearly got your cousin injured,' he insisted. 'You've precipitated a crisis, just when I had everything under control.'

'I don't understand. What's happening?'

'The river,' Matt informed her calmly, changing course and making for the window, Carrie still securely against his chest, 'now flows through Falconridge. It burst its banks.'

He took her to the window, never putting her down and she looked out at devastation. The sun was shining, the sky was blue but where yesterday there had been parkland, now there was the brown swirling water of the river. Everything except the trees and the tallest bushes seemed to be submerged and she could see Allan's car down by the front of the house, the flood water almost to its roof.

'Your cousin sacrificed his car for the greater good of all,' Matt informed her dramatically. 'Back to bed now, there's nothing else to see.'

'Oh, Matt!' Her sympathy suddenly brought a grin to his face.

'No problem. The cars are in the stable block and it's clearly not going to get that far. It's stopped rising. There are firms to see to the cleaning and drying that's going to be needed and, thanks to Allan, we had a warning. Everything's going to be all right, providing you agree to stop popping out at us and causing trouble.'

'I can't understand why you're not really upset about it,' Carrie said, looking at him and then taking another look at the swirling water. 'Everything must be ruined, there are so many beautiful things here. I couldn't bear it if—if . . . '

'Does Falconridge mean so much to you?' he asked quietly.

'It's a lovely house,' she said quickly, looking away from his intent eyes. 'I mean, all the things you've gathered here are so important.'

'I use to think so,' he agreed softly, suddenly looking weary again. 'Anyway, it's home to the twins and they seem to be happy here, at least. But there'll be little sign of damage when the cleaners have been in. As I say, we had a warning.'

He turned back to the bed, his momentary interest in her thoughts and pleasures fading.

'What now, Matt?' Allan asked tiredly from the doorway, his hand still on Vivienne's shoulder. Matt stopped in mid-stride.

'If you two can wade into the kitchen and make tea, we'll all take tea with Lady Caroline and discuss our adventures.'

It took all the tension from the air in a way that only Matt could and Carrie looked at Vivienne in her strange garb with womanly sympathy.

'Oh, Vivienne!' To her relief and surprise, Vivienne burst into peals of laughter, looking down at her appearance, her eyes sparkling.

'Neat, eh? This has been the most exciting day of my life.'

'Come on,' Allan ordered, shaking his head in disbelief, and Matt settled Carrie back in bed, sinking tiredly into a nearby chair.

'The story so far, as you no doubt intend to get every last item. We decided to stop work early because we'd done very well and I was pretty tired. Allan was just getting into his car to drive back to London when he looked across the park and saw the first trickle of water come over the bank. So then we all moved fast.

Ruby put the girls on the window seat in my room to watch the river and keep them out of mischief and we moved everything that we could in the time we had, about twenty minutes. Then it came like a tidal wave. Luckily it had a few obstacles in its path and luckily too, the house is on a slight rise, so it's about level with the second step of the stairs and we have been able to get things out that stand on legs, tables and so forth. We've been carting things upstairs ever since painfully!

'The twins are still glued to the look-out post, they've even had lunch there, and we've still got heating up here from the emergency generator, but none downstairs. Ruby's a miracle, she dished up lunch on the old camping stove, she'll be wanting her backwoodsman's badge now I expect.'

'Oh, Matt! Your beautiful house!' she said with sympathy but he looked at her sternly.

'Our beautiful house, Carrie!' he corrected, with the first sign of harshness he had shown.

Allan and Vivienne came in with a tray, laughing over some private joke, and Carrie sat up in bed feeling like Alice in Wonderland. Nothing was as it had been. Allan and Vivienne were friendly to each other, Matt and Allan talked easily together and Miss Trevere of the morning had now become Vivienne. Carrie might well have felt excluded but Matt gave up his seat to Vivienne and sat on the bed, leaning back against the headboard and after a while, his arm came slowly and gently around Carrie's shoulders. It was tentative almost, as if he expected a rebuff, but she longed to be close to him, her illness, her bewilderment and her love making her snuggle against his arm regardless of what anyone thought, and she felt the shudder of a sigh run through him as he pulled her closer.

All in all, it was the happiest hour that Carrie had spent for a very long time and it became clear, as

Matt and Allan discussed the problem, that as soon
as the water had receded sufficiently to make it possible, they would all have to move out and drive back
to London. Matt's greatest concern was Carrie's state
of health and the possibility of the upstairs heating
breaking down. Luckily, the Mercedes and Vivienne's
smaller car were well clear. It only needed the water
level on the drive to drop and they could all go.

It had fallen by morning and in a hazy sunshine,
Carrie feeling much better and well wrapped up, the
twins wide-eyes and excited, they all went through the
mud that was now covering most of the downstairs
and out by the back door to the cars.

'I'll drive, Allan,' Vivienne said with bright determination. 'What with suitcases, people and dolls, you'll
need all the Mercedes to yourselves.'

'Thank you, no!' Allan rejoined with equal determination, taking her keys. 'I'll drive you! I've never
been suicidal and I've got a lot of life in me yet.'

The remark pleased Vivienne enormously and with
Matt's car in the lead, the little convoy set off carefully
to the main road, Ruby and the twins on the back
seat, Carrie beside Matt, almost hidden by a car rug
that he had wrapped around her to the great amusement of Gemma and Pippa.

On the outskirts of the city, the two cars went their
separate ways and Matt continued on towards the
flat. In spite of her 'flu, Carrie's spirits were high.
Suddenly it seemed that things were better. Allan and
Matt were on first name terms, some kind of understanding clearly reached. Matt's affection for the
children was in no doubt and his recent behaviour
towards herself could almost be described as tender.

But the flat had been a milestone in her life. It was
here that she had placed her future trustingly, lovingly
in Matt's hands. It was here that he had worshipped
her, made her part of himself, and she wondered if
she could face the familiar rooms with her new-found

knowledge. She fell silent and Matt, after one brief glance at her tight and anxious face, seemed to lose the buoyancy that had made their departure from Falconridge an adventure instead of a retreat.

'You can drop me here, Mr Silver.' Ruby's voice cut into Carrie's anxious throughts. 'I've only the one case and there's taxis on the corner.'

'Where are you going?' Carrie even heard the panic in her own voice as Matt swung in to the kerb.

'My sister's, Miss Caroline. I thought you knew. There's not enough room in the flat for all of us.'

'Of course not, sorry.' She should have realised. There were only two bedrooms.

Unexpectedly, Ruby hugged and kissed the twins, promising that they would all be together again in just over a week, as Carrie sat in frozen shock. Two bedrooms! One with twin beds—the guest room which would be for the twins—and one with a wide comfortable bed, Matt's room, their room, where Matt had taught her all that love could offer. There were no other bedrooms.

'I'll see you soon, Miss Caroline. Take care. Fancy, a week's holiday right out of the blue! I'll get those sweaters for the twins finished while I'm sitting talking.'

She went and Matt pulled back into the traffic, his own face still and shuttered. It didn't need much reasoning to follow where Carrie's thoughts had flown and he clearly did not like her sudden silence, her vague replies to Ruby.

'Will—will it be cold in the flat?' she asked, more for something to say than for any desire for information.

'No. The heating comes on automatically at set intervals when the flat's unoccupied. I'll set the timer for normal use as soon as we get in.' He never even glanced at her and his eyes on the traffic never flickered in her direction. There was a dreadful watchfulness about him, a keyed-up waiting, tension in his body like a spring ready to snap and Carrie sank deeper into her fears and worries, slowly sinking back into misery.

He loaded their cases into the lift in the underground car park and they shot up in silent luxury to his apartment, the twins quiet for once, no questions, and Carrie's eyes downcast as she waited for Matt to make the first move.

There was a pile of mail inside the hall and Matt simply picked it up and dropped it carelessly on the table.

'Aren't you going to look through it?' Carrie asked, seeing his apparent unconcern.

'Later. All the mail is forwarded to Falconridge. These are either circulars or people who don't know where I am. There are few of those, so they can wait. In here, girls.'

He took the big suitcase that the twins shared through into the guest bedroom and Carrie felt reluctant to step further into the flat than the hall. Sooner or later, probably sooner, Matt would raise the question of their own sleeping arrangements and she didn't know what to say. There had been too much love in that room to face anything but the bliss of the past and the past was over. Here, it would be all too apparent; here, she would remember that first time.

Her eyes stared vaguely at the pile of mail tossed haphazardly on to the polished table. Everything inside her froze, turned cold. Only the corner of the letter was visible, but it was visible enough to see the stamp. America! She gave no thought to any of Matt's business affairs, letters of that nature went to the head office and it wasn't that kind of an envelope. It was private, personal and her mind said only one thing—Yvette.

'Do you want to help the girls or don't you feel up to it?' Matt stood in the doorway leading from the bedroom, his eyes watchful and cool. 'While we're here, we'll get our main meals sent up. We'll manage breakfast.'

'I can do the cooking,' Carrie said, not meeting his eyes.

'There's no reason why you should. Influenza tends to drag on if you neglect it. They've promised to have Falconridge ready in about ten days, we'll survive.'

She didn't answer. Instead she began to walk slowly towards the girls' bedroom but she never got there. Matt took her arm and swung her none too gently into the other room, closing the door.

'You can relax,' he rasped bitterly. 'This is your room. You can bring your clothes and your memories and settle in here with your own quiet ghost. I'll be sleeping in the sitting-room. There's a long settee as you no doubt remember and there are plenty of blankets. A few days there will be less traumatic then lying on the edge of this bed watching you dream. I'll have less of a cold feeling inside me. If you talk to him in your sleep, I won't even know!'

He went out and she hardly dare look around the room. Everywhere there was Matt's voice, deep, quiet, warm. Everywhere there was the memory of enchantment, of her girlhood changed so tenderly to womanhood. If Falconridge had spelled the end of her life, then here was the beginning.

She went to help the girls and when she came back, her suitcase was on the bed, Matt's nowhere to be seen. He intended to live separately even in such confined surroundings. He disregarded any discomfort and had resumed his former role of victor in a business deal, except that they were all losing. Maybe now with a letter to tempt him he would go back to Yvette, if only for a while, and she couldn't face the prospect.

It was clearly an effort for him to speak to any of them but he managed with the girls. There was a television for the evenings, there were books, records and the small distraction of the two waiters who came at intervals from the nearby hotel and served their meals. After that there was bed. Carrie to the wide warmth of the bed in Matt's room and Matt left reading, his face sombre and still, his eyes firmly on the printed pages. She never even dared to say good-night and the letter had gone.

For several days, the situation held, Carrie hardly daring to breathe, expecting any day to find Matt packing to fly to Florida, her health back to normal but her depression growing daily, and tension visibly mounting inside Matt until he seemed ready to explode. Even the twins fell silent until Matt decided to alter their desperate little situation.

He phoned to see if the crates of toys had arrived. They had. As they were in London, delivery was promised for that day and Carrie thought that at least unpacking them would give her something to do. There was little work in the flat and what little there was Matt seemed to have done every day before she got up. He seemed to be up no matter how early she was until she began to think that he must spend the whole night reading. At any rate, he looked drawn and pale as if he had been the one to be ill rather than she.

CHAPTER EIGHT

THE crates arrived soon after lunch and excitement ran high as far as Gemma and Pippa were concerned. Their small jean-clad figures constantly on the move, they helped to empty the big packing cases when Matt had prised off the lids, and in an endless trail they ferried the smaller packages to the sitting-room.

Even though Carrie spent most of her time on her knees helping, Matt managed to avoid her eyes and succeeded in being excited with the twins while being completely cold with her. She had never felt lonelier. He spoke only once, and that in surprise.

'Is this all? There are no other crates to come?'

'No,' she looked away quickly, 'we didn't gather a lot of things—well, it was never really home—I mean . . . ' She didn't know what to say, she understood his surprise. Most of the things in the crates belonged to the twins—books, toys, games—and very little to her. There was nothing of Kevin Haley there, no token of her supposed happiness, no photograph, not even one little thing to remind her.

'I'll clear this up,' she said quietly and Matt nodded, his eyes meeting hers squarely, a keen intelligence gleaming from narrowed lids.

'Push the packing back into the crates, I'll get it moved to the garage.'

He stood and went in to the excited girls as Carrie too stood up on legs that were trembling. It was a hurdle that she had taken badly but when the crates had been packed, she had no idea that they would be opened in front of Matt. She had not expected ever to

140

see him again, and as the thought came into her head so did Grandma Ellie's voice: 'Count your blessings every day.'

For the rest of her life, she would be Matt's wife, the mother of his two beautiful children. Every day she would see him, hear his voice, know the odd moment of tenderness. Maybe that was all she had been entitled to in this life, and she counted her blessings. She was alive, breathing the same air as Matt, able to hold his children close, and suddenly her spirits lifted on wings, her depression easing away as if it had never been.

She was just going in to sort out the wave of chaos that had hit the beautiful sitting-room, her task in the hall completed, when Pippa's voice held her, scared and worried, in the doorway.

'Look! All my birthday cards!'

'And mine!' Gemma dived into the bag that Pippa had unearthed and there they were, all the cards that they had saved meticulously. They began to go through them, remembering with horrifying ease who had sent them. 'That's from Maggie and that's from Ross and . . . ' Matt was busy picking up bits of paper and Carrie relaxed, ready to join him, the sight of his bent head, his capable hands making her heart turn over, but Pippa's next words nearly made her heart stop.

'When is June the eighth, Daddy?'

'June the eighth?' Matt sat back on his heels and thought about it. 'Let's see, about seven weeks away.' He turned back to his task but Pippa pounced on him gleefully.

'It's our birthday then!'

'You can't remember things like that,' he assured her with a laugh. 'Even you, my pet, can't be that clever.'

'I do!' Pippa asserted. 'Uncle Allan taught us. He said we should be able to write our names and remember our birthdays or we'd look silly when we went to school.'

'Really?' Matt turned with interest and Carrie walked out into the kitchen, her heart thumping, hearing, as she went, Gemma's voice saying in triumph, 'Uncle Allan wrote it on the back of our cards. Look, it says here!'

'So it does. June the eighth. Well, well.' Matt's voice was a deep murmur and Carrie hurried into the kitchen, closing the door and trying to still her thumping heart.

'A lie will find you out. It flies round like a bird and comes back to sit on your shoulder.' Her grandmother's voice seemed to be ringing in her ears and she jumped guiltily as Matt came silently into the kitchen.

'Making some coffee?' he asked soberly, his eyes glancing across at her as he put a pile of waste paper into the rubbish bin.

'Yes—yes. I'll get some milk for the girls too.'

'Good idea.' He turned to leave and his utter nonchalance told her better than any violent words that he had worked out the deceit. He knew. He just wasn't going to mention it.

'Matt!' Suddenly she just couldn't face the strain any more, the way they were like strangers when they had once loved so deeply, the way he had taken the blow of the knowledge and ridden the punch with no emotion. They were systematically destroying each other until there would be no feelings in either of them towards anyone. And she felt the guilt deeply. At Falconridge, before the flood and after, Matt had relaxed into a sort of tentative gentleness. Whatever his reasons, he had to have that peace back again. Now, he looked haggard, tired and alone and she couldn't let that go on.

He stopped as she spoke and looked at her calmly,

his eyes merely polite and she started to tell him, her own face pale.

'Matt, the girls are . . . Gemma and Pippa are . . . '

'Are mine,' he finished for her. 'I know. I've known since I took my first close look at them on the day we were married.' He was speaking with devastatingly cold control and she stared at him for a second.

'But . . . But you couldn't . . . '

'Since I began to shave at an early age,' he remarked evenly, 'I've been looking into the mirror with boring regularity. One recognises one's own eyes after a while, it becomes part of a built-in pattern. When two pairs of eyes exactly the same looked back at me, knowledge and understanding came hand in hand at once.'

'You—you never said . . . ' She looked away from the coolly controlled gaze but he moved close and tilted her face up, forcing her to meet his eyes.

'And neither did you, Carrie,' he said quietly. 'All I have to thank you for is that you at least allowed me to behave like their father even if I was supposed to be less entitled to their love than Allan. Now, however, I begin to see why Haley is so wonderful in your eyes, so firmly alive your heart. You were pregnant when you walked out of Falconridge and he shouldered the burden. I've never even thought about it before. I suppose I didn't want to, it's funny how things you don't want to know are frequently pushed under your nose. I salute him!'

His hand fell away and he said coldly as if the matter of the twins was now dismissed for ever, 'Tonight, there is a dinner. I expect you to attend as a dutiful wife. Allan has agreed to babysit. Be ready for seven-thirty and behave as a wife would normally be seen to behave!'

At seven o'clock, Allan arrived and Carrie was not unduly surprised to see Vivienne with him.

'I've brought my own long-playing record,' he said

wryly, indicating Vivienne. 'I hope you don't mind? She can do the more menial tasks.'

'Splendid!' Matt ushered them into the now immaculate sitting-room.' We shan't be late. The girls are asleep. Anything you want, simply root around and find it.'

'You look lovely, Carrie,' Allan said, smiling across at her, and she managed to keep up a bright chatter until they were ready to leave.

Her image in the bedroom mirror startled her as she went in to pick up her wrap. The coffee-coloured dress suited her, its thin straps glittering with dark brown sequins, the flowing georgette gown whispering over the silken skirt, her hair burnished to dark gold in the lamplight. She looked good, but her startled glance at herself had nothing to do with admiration, she could hardly believe that she looked exactly the same. Inside she felt dead, cold and utterly beaten. Matt's cheerful greeting to Allan and Vivienne had been the only words he had spoken since the afternoon.

It was the sort of dinner she had attended many times with Matt and she went with no misgivings, too cold and numb inside for anything to touch her now. There were the usual tables for four around the great sweep of the floor, the huge room reserved for a symposium of the wealthy and influential. Here, though, there would be no open discussion, no one person putting views to the assembled guests. Here, things would be conducted as they were conducted in Ancient Greece, a dinner, drinks and convivial chatter, chatter that would determine the future of many firms, produce heartbreak or astounded joy.

She wondered how Allan could ever have hoped to survive in this sort of world and she knew that he would not have been able to. He would now, though, and he would climb into these exalted circles because Matt had taken him under his wing as he had once taken her. The wing that sheltered Allan, though, was one of iron.

Matt was power, influence, cold-headed ruthlessness, and she entered the room in a very different status from the one she had occupied when she had come to a similar gathering to support Allan. Eyes looked at them and looked away. People were affable but not inquisitive. Tall and handsome, elegantly dressed, Matt escorted her to their table, nodding and smiling as the mood took him, untouched by any anxieties, whereas Allan had been ready to take any blow that befell him.

She was glad to see John Carmichael and his wife Sylvia at their table; at least there would be civilised conversation and Matt would unbend a little while they were in the public eye.

The dinner progressed easily enough. Matt and John talked together about the firm and Matt's other interests, while Sylvia questioned Carrie about the twins, the flood at Falconridge, and kept up a steady flow of news that stretched back over four years.

Although she could not be said by any means to be enjoying herself, at least Carrie felt that this was better than the silence of the flat, and she sat alone quite contentedly as John and Sylvia danced and Matt left the table with quick excuse to her as someone signalled him from across the floor.

It was then that she heard the voice that made her toes curl in her shoes: Cynthia, Lady Welland, the wife of another of Matt's associates. Carrie turned with a fixed, glassy smile to face what she knew instinctively would be an attack.

She knew that Cynthia Welland must be at least seventy-five or six but she had none of the grace or gentleness that should come with age. Her forte was gossip, preferably malicious, and she sank into the seat vacated by Matt, her clear, cold eyes agleam, to make the most of her good fortune in getting Carrie alone.

'Caroline, my dear, it's lovely to see you back with Matt. We thought it was all over finally. You look well.'

Fascinated as ever by the over-painted face, the enormous fluff of blonded hair, the weight of diamonds that seemed to be too much for the deceptively fragile frame, Carrie only said, 'Thank you.'

'I hear that you have children, two little girls? What a man Matt is to take all three of you on. He's such a dear boy. I've known him for years and I'm afraid he always had these soft spots, these little blind spots.'

Carrie felt stunned, staring in disbelief at this poisonous little speech delivered with the skill of an actress.

'The girls belong to Matt, Lady Cynthia, and he loves them very much. I would hardly call his affection for them a blind spot.'

'Of course, dear.' The talon-like fingers patted Carrie's hand. 'I'm sure you misunderstood me. He's had a hard life, you know, even as a boy and I have a deep concern for him. I knew his father really well,' she added, a spice in her voice that was a forerunner of further malice. 'Did you know that Matt's father was a vicar? A parish priest? Of course, he had no time for Matthew. We were none of us surprised when he never came home after Cambridge, never even attended his father's funeral. He was far too happy in America, you know. I mean, we could all tell at a glance when he came back. He was so contented, so sure of himself, so prosperous, heaven knows why he ever came back. It's the only happiness he's ever had, they say he still keeps in touch with her.'

'With whom?' Carrie asked as coldly as she could, her hands in her lap to still the trembling.

'Why, surely you know, Caroline dear? The woman

he knew so well before he—took you on. We were so surprised, I mean you were so different from what Matthew had been used to, a mere little waif and apparently she's beautiful, wealthy and I believe,' she lowered her voice for extra drama, 'quite well known.'

Feeling as many had felt before her that there was no way of answering Lady Welland's outrageous rudeness and malice except by a hard blow, Carrie sat shaken and stunned, her feelings verging on hysteria. She wanted to scream at her, to call her an old witch, to order her away but she could do nothing. As usual, there was the spark of truth in her remarks and the skill of embroidering of this spark had been perfected during years of practice.

'Carrie, care to dance?' John Carmichael hovered over her and she almost leapt out of her seat in her eagerness to escape.

'I see you encountered trouble,' he observed quietly when they were safely out among the other dancing couples. 'Sylvia pointed out your pale face and your ghastly companion and I charged to the rescue. Sylvia refuses to return until Lady Cynthia leaves.'

'Thank you, John,' she managed through trembling lips. 'She's a horrible old woman. I'll never go to another function if she's there, no matter what Matt says.'

Matt's hand came to her shoulder and John Carmichael looked at him with an unusual little flicker of annoyance.

'Were you signalling to me, John?'

'I was! Caroline had just had the very unpleasant task of speaking to, or rather listening to, Lady Cynthia. I feel, Matt, that she needs holding a little more tightly than I can in all decency manage. Yes! I did signal you!'

He handed Carrie over to Matt and walked off to find Sylvia. Even the back of his neck looked pink and angry and Carrie felt a burst of gratitude for his protection.

As Matt took her into his arms and moved into the rhythm of the dance, he felt her trembling. He could hardly have avoided noticing, as she was shaking so much.

'What the hell has that old witch been saying to you?' he demanded angrily, drawing back and looking into her white face.

She couldn't answer, she lowered her eyes and shook her head wanting to run out and hide. She didn't want to be told about Yvette, she knew about her, she knew that Matt had been happy with her or he would not have rushed away when she wrote. Her position as his wife was the result of his violent anger, his thirst for revenge and even now he was probably regretting it, longing to be back with Yvette and waking up to the fact that he had tied himself to Carrie. How long could he last out before he decided to go? What had the latest letter said?

She drew a deep shuddering breath and her head fell forward in defeat, her legs hardly able to support her.

'My God! I'll kill that woman!' Matt pulled her tightly into his arms, more supporting her than dancing with her, his face against her hair as her head sank to his chest.

'Do you want to leave, Carrie?' he asked quietly enough but she could feel rage boiling inside him.

'I—I think I must. I'm sorry, Matt.'

'Never mind. Never mind.' He must have signalled to John Carmichael because he appeared like an angry unwilling genie at Matt's side.

'I'm taking Carrie home, John. Thanks for the rescue. I'll not be in the office for a few days but you have one priority job. Delve deeply into the affairs of the Wellands. He doesn't concern me, he's merely an old fool, but I want her off the board of any company that she's on. If she's on any committee, even a local jumble sale, I want her off it. It's time she was put out to pasture!'

The 'hard, cold voice, edged with rage merely had John nodding silently, but there was a certain satisfaction in his voice when he said quietly, 'My pleasure. Goodnight.'

She was still shaking, still reeling from the trauma, when they were in the car and Matt looked across at her, his face expressionless.

'Want to tell me about it?' he asked, as he had done once before so long ago.

'No.' She shook her head and then because she couldn't help it she blurted out, 'She was hinting that the girls weren't yours, that you'd taken us all in from pity, from the goodness of your heart. She said . . . '

'Go on.' He was seething with a wicked temper and she stared at her clenched hands.

'Nothing else much really,' she whispered, 'except she said your father was a vicar and he had no time for you. She said you had only ever been happy in America and that I was a surprise to everyone because I was a—a . . . '

She couldn't go on and she doubted if Matt would have let her. He started the car and drove out of the hotel car park into the road, his face like granite, his eyes glittering with fury and spoke not another word.

Allan was reading when they got back, Vivienne curled up on the settee fast asleep.

'You're early!' he observed in surprise. 'Hope you weren't worried about the twins, they're sleeping like angels.'

'Carrie wasn't too well,' Matt said quietly making a great effort to be normal. 'Too soon after the 'flu. I should have known better. What's this, then?' he added looking at Vivienne.

'She talked herself into a coma,' Allan grinned. 'The needle stuck I think. I'll stir her to life.' He shook her shoulder and she blinked and sat up, looking just a tiny bit sheepish.

'I haven't really been asleep,' she offered lamely.

'You've been asleep for over an hour,' Allan assured her, adding slyly, 'snoring like the proverbial.'

'I never have! Oh, did I? I don't! It's not true!'

'You'll never know, will you?' Allan laughed helping her to her feet. 'Come on, let's get a late supper at Dino's.'

Carrie was glad they were going. She only wanted to get away by herself, to hide in the wide bed and never lift her head again.

'Carrie!' Matt called when she walked out as soon as the door had closed behind Allan and Vivienne, but she didn't answer and he let her go.

She heard him go along to the shower as she lay cold and trembling in bed, her shock and misery beginning to well up into heartbroken tears and when he passed the door on his way back, she hid her face in the pillow to silence the sounds of her unhappiness.

There was no one to turn to, no one to tell. Allan was happy now, his future secure, and she would hold the pain in her own heart rather than burden him with her new and endless miseries. There was no one else, nobody in the whole world.

She was suddenly lifted from the pillows, her body, shaking with deep, harsh sobs, pulled tightly into strong warm arms as Matt sat on the bed beside her, switching on the light and refusing to let her go.

He said nothing, simply held her tightly, his hand strong and gentle on her head as he pressed her to his shoulder and stroked soothingly through her curls.

It took a long time to stop crying and even then she wouldn't look at him, even then she tried to pull away, but he would have none of that. He cupped her unhappy face in warm hands, looking deeply into her tear-filled eyes before his lips covered hers, warm and firm, domineering, possessive and relentless.

'Now!' he said when the kiss had stilled her grief and the final dry sobs were ended. 'Now, I'll tell you some facts, except they won't be cooked up from malice and they won't be designed to cause you pain.

'Yes, you were a surprise to everybody, a shock, even, because they knew me, Carrie, they knew my cold-blooded heart, my drive to be top, my soulless determination. Then you appeared on my arm, gentle, innocent, guileless, childlike and untouchable. I imagine they thought that I was out for fun, a new experience to brighten my hardbitten days and I imagine that some of the ladies of my acquaintance got together for jolly tongue-wagging sessions, damned annoyed that they weren't at Falconridge.'

He looked at her with eyes like topaz, clear and bright, full of purpose.

'I told you it should never have been me. I told you I'd tried to keep away from you. I was no innocent, Carrie. I was nearly fourteen hard years older than you, with women in my life and a brain as coldly calculating as one of Allan's computers. But I'd seen you and it was too late. The fact that I went crazy when I lost you, the fact that you're back here as my wife with my children has flipped them totally, and they're searching around for little bits of news so that they can be proved to have been right after all. Cynthia Welland is merely the instrument, the one with the nerve to speak. These people are not my friends, Carrie. They're nothing! You know and I know that Gemma and Pippa are mine. You know I love them.'

He watched her for a few seconds and when she didn't speak, when she continued to gaze at him silently, he took a handful of her curls, rocking her head gently from side to side.

'What else was there?' he murmured, his eyes warm and gentle. 'Oh, yes, my father. True he was a vicar and true he had little time for me, but that didn't

mean that we loved each other any less. He was
wrapped up in the church, in the parish, it was the
only way he could cope with life after my mother
died. From the age of eleven when my mother died, I
had Ruby when she became housekeeper, I had school
and I had nothing else. I never did intend to go back
after I left Cambridge, except for visits, and as it
happened, I never even attended his funeral. I was in
New York and I was in hospital. Happy in America?
I was successful, I learned what power was, I learned
not to be vulnerable. You were my happiness! You!'

She couldn't think clearly, couldn't divorce the lies
from the truth and she shook her head in despair,
trying to find some sure foothold for belief, remembering his race to Florida, his cruel rage when he
found her again, his silent recognition of the twins.

Don't shake your head!' He ordered with a sudden
flare of anger. 'You know it's true!'

She could only stare at him with empty eyes, frightened to be receptive once again. For a short time at
Falconridge she had stepped back into an offered
happiness, she had readily accepted the tenderness
that Matt had seemed to show only to find herself in
the position of facing his savage remarks, his cold
indifference since they had moved here.

Like a frightened animal she simply kept quiet,
certain that anything she said, any move she made
would bring only trouble, trouble that she couldn't
face.

He had no intention of waiting for her to reach any
conclusion or make any move, because for a few
seconds, he stared into her empty eyes, his own eyes
darkening with anger and frustration and then he
caught her to him with a grip that seemed designed to
be deliberately painful.

Her opportunity to speak was gone. He had made
a decision of his own and her gasp of fear was stifled
by fiercely demanding lips. His kisses seemed to be

calculated to pull her into the world he saw, the world he wanted, whether she wished to come or not. They were a punishment and a warning and he gave her no time to react other than with fear.

His hands didn't relax their grip even when he pushed her to the deep softness of the bed, his body covering hers instantly, quelling her struggles to be free as she became aware of what was happening. He kissed her endlessly until all her will began to ebb away, until the room seemed unreal and her world one of pain and panic. He had never treated her like this before, had never shown her any glimpse of his physical strength, but now that strength was subduing her and through the panic, she felt the inexorable rise of excitement, the inescapable and instinctive longing to soften in his angry arms.

As swiftly as it had arisen, his anger seemed to fall away, his body relaxing in its determined drive to subjugate her by force and his hands began to stroke her, to seek the swollen curves of her breasts as he felt her reaction.

'You want this, Carrie,' he breathed softly, his thumbs probing her breasts, lingering to urge the aroused nipples to further excitement. 'You want this in any way it comes.'

His voice was cold, calculating, triumphant and her eyes flickered open to find him looking down at her through narrowed, darkened eyes.

'Not a word to say?' he queried, softly mocking. 'You're afraid to admit to being alive, to wanting me?'

'I don't!' She couldn't quell the little gasp of pain and pleasure as his thumbs probed more deeply, and his soft laughter sent a further shiver of apprehension through her body.

'Let's find out,' he suggested in a deep whisper, his hands sliding the thin nightdress away as he cupped the silken skin of her breast, his mouth claiming it with a driving urgency that shot feeling through her like the sparks from a roaring fire. 'Now, Carrie,' he invited. 'Deny it now.'

He was treating her as he never treated her before, with no gentleness, no tenderness, only a towering, masculine urge to drive her into submission. His taunting voice had her renewing her struggles, panting for breath, desperately fighting the insidious lethargy that seemed to be claiming her limbs.

'No! I . . . ' Her voice was roughly silenced by lips that burned her, her frantic hands gripped by one powerful hand as the other peeled away her night-dress.

'Yes, Carrie!' he ground out against her lips as his free hand began to move over her, to find all the places that he seemed to remember so well, all the nerve endings that could melt her in his arms. His ferocity subsided as she moved against him with the inevitability of someone who is submitting to a pre-ordained fate. It was Matt, she loved him, wanted him, she had never wanted anyone else and his arms relaxed, his hands gentled as he freed her wrists and pulled her even closer, shrugging out of his robe and moulding her to the hard power of his body.

He raised his head at last and looked down at her, totally in control of her, waiting for her eyes to open and meet his heated, narrowed gaze. He threaded his finger through her hair forcing her head up until she was arched beneath him like the vanquished before a conqueror.

'It's time you were pregnant again,' he said coolly, stressing every word, gripping her tightly as alarm flared again at the coldness of his words. 'Don't waste any energy in fighting,' he advised quietly, 'it's going to happen. With my child inside you, you'll feel less inclined to hang on to a wonderful, lost dream. I can't think of anything more real and intrusive for a woman than the knowledge that she's carrying someone's child. My child, Carrie! Reality!'

'No!' She stared at him in a sort of fascinated horror. 'I won't! You wouldn't . . . '

Slowly he allowed his weight to lower to her until every hard, thrusting muscle of his body seemed to be speaking to everything inside her. His hand in her hair moved to stroke her shoulder, to sweep across the tender skin of the breast that had so recently known the savagery of his mouth, to slide along her thigh and beneath her to lift her closer.

'I want you,' he murmured deeply. 'That's one thing that never stops being real. I want you and nothing is going to prevent me from having you tonight.'

She twisted frantically, frightened at the cold-blooded assertion but she was trapped by his strength, helpless beneath him and as his lips claimed hers in a deep, drowning kiss, her cries of fright slowly changed to whimpers of desire until the tight grip on her relaxed and he moved against her with a growing urgency that added fuel to the fire of her own excitement.

When her excitement was at its peak, he lifted his head, looking down at her with glittering eyes, his body restless and impatient.

'You're mine, Carrie!' he rasped harshly. 'I'll not let you slide again into your grey half-world. After tonight you'll know you're alive.'

'Matt!' Her desperate little plea, emphasised by her searching hands, her mouth eager to be claimed again, brought a flare of possessive fire into his eyes.

'Ask me!' he demanded thickly. 'Tell me what you want! Let's have no mistake, no denial tomorrow. Ask me!'

'Love me, Matt!' She pleaded, her hands moving over his hard chest, his smooth shoulders. 'Oh, please love me, Matt,' she sobbed.

'Love you?' he muttered, his face taut with passion, his body poised to possess her. 'You imagine I would dare? Loving you threw me into hell. Don't expect me to return to that.'

For a second, fear raced through her, threatening and dark, but her need for him rose over it and she lay sobbing quietly in his arms, her heated body speaking for her, gasping with shock and delight as he suddenly possessed her, his groan of satisfaction against her lips.

'Is this what you want?' he asked thickly, 'to be back where it all began? Except that I worshipped you and every time I took you it was like a prayer, a blessing. What is it now, Carrie?'

'Don't! Oh, Matt, don't speak like that!' Her tears flowed even though the excitement and longing winged through her.

'Oh, God! Carrie! Carrie!'

Suddenly, unexpectedly, miraculously, he was gentle, tender. His driving urge slowing to a coaxing desire to please her, and her desolation melted away as he kissed her eyes, kissing away the tears, stroking her hair, murmuring words of comfort that she couldn't recognise except for their familiarity and a remembrance of the first time this room.

Finally they lay spent and quiet in each others arms and Matt stirred, moving aside, lying on his back to stare at the ceiling, his face almost gaunt.

'Matt.' Tentatively, she touched his shoulder but a shudder ran through him that dispelled the lingering magic like a blast of cold air.

'Don't touch me, Carrie!' He felt for his robe and stood, tying it around him before he turned to look at her.

'Didn't I tell you that nowadays you bring out every bit of savagery that's deep inside me?' he asked bitterly. 'I came here to comfort you, to silence those pitiful sobs that I could hear as I passed the door. I ended up raping you!'

'It wasn't . . . . ' she began, trembling with reaction

and the shock of his hard voice.

'It didn't end like that, but the intention was there. Don't imagine that it wasn't!' he bit out in harsh self-loathing. 'I wanted to make you pregnant, even against your will. I started off with every intention of hurting you if necessary to achieve that end and, God forgive me, I still hope it's happened!'

He walked out, closing the door, leaving her bruised and shocked, the warmth and happiness vanishing, too stunned for tears, too unhappy to go over in her mind the implication of his words.

She pulled the sheets over her head, curling in a self-protecting ball of misery, shivering with pain and exhaustion as sleep claimed her at last.

CHAPTER NINE

MATT was nowhere to be seen when Carrie got up next morning. She had no idea whether he had simply gone out because he couldn't bear to see her or if he had gone into the office. As far as she knew, she would have to face the day with only the twins for company, watching the door and jumping in alarm every time the phone rang. It was a prospect that she didn't exactly relish, she was nervous enough as it was after last night and she had no intention of facing the girls with this kind of atmosphere any longer. They had not had a father when they lived in Australia but they had been used to the constant affection and good humour of Allan. Very soon this atmosphere would begin to get to them; if Ruby had noticed it sufficiently to begin to threaten to leave, then the children would quickly pick up the unhappy vibrations.

Brightly, smiling and purposeful, she dressed them for an outing and, calling a taxi, took them on a shopping spree, their first. There were lots of things to see, shops that would make their eyes open wide and although it was not possible to buy happiness, at least it would dull the edge of misery and take their minds off the growing gloom that seemed to surround Matt.

As expeditions went, it was only a limited success. The traffic was heavy and a little frightening. She was used to having Allan with her to help with the two small girls who both wanted to be lifted simultaneously to see into windows and on to counters that were far too high to enjoy in any other way and Carrie soon found herself hot and tired.

'Up we go!' She suddenly found Sylvia Carmichael with her, hauling Gemma up to gaze on to the display in a window as Carrie lifted Pippa. 'You need a big pram with an automatic lifting device.' Sylvia laughed as Carrie turned to her gratefully. 'You also need a coffee. Upstairs, all!'

'You're the most welcome bully that I've met today,' Carrie said with a heartfelt sigh as they settled later in the upstairs restaurant. 'I'm so used to having another adult with me to help to heave the twins about, it's been quite an experience to cope alone.'

'Matt should be with you, but I see he's in the office today.'

'Is he?' Carrie asked dully, no longer able to keep up a normal public face.

'Well, I expect so. He almost knocked me over when I was leaving. I'd been to see John and I was just going out when Matt steamed in. He didn't apologise either, the brute.' She looked at the twins and then looked back to Carrie, lowering her voice. 'Thing aren't going too well, are they, Carrie?'

'No.' Carrie sat with her coffee-cup in both hands, worried that she would drop it if any sudden noise came. Her nerves were on edge and she seemed to be constantly trembling nowadays.

'Is it anything to do with Cynthia Welland's remarks last night? No, don't answer that, it's none of my business. But neither you nor Matt seem to be back in the rosy glow of old.'

'It's all right,' Carrie said listlessly. 'I suppose Lady Welland just brought things more into the open.'

She found herself telling Sylvia about the poisonous remarks and her friend's face flushed with annoyance.

'The nasty old witch!'

The twins had left the table to wander across to the high window and now they stood enthralled seeing London before and below them. Both Carrie and

Sylvia turned their chairs to keep a better eye on them and for a few minutes they had privacy.

'There was a woman in America before you came into Matt's life, Carrie,' Sylvia remarked quietly. 'I know that because John was unusually intrigued. Matt used to ring her quite a lot when he was building up the London office, but gradually as the the business became more and more London-based, he called less frequently. She called him sometimes, though. I should think that he might have phoned her from the flat but most of the calls seemed to be about business as far as anyone knew. It's always been a source of deep interest when and whom Matt would finally settle down with. Anyway, if it was a love affair, it was before your time and certainly conducted over a long distance because when a trip to New York was necessary it was John who had to make it. Matt never went.'

'Maybe that's because she's in Florida,' Carrie observed bitterly.

'I see. Well, I know Matt didn't go there either because he worked here like a lunatic. I wasn't surprised when Rosemary left. For a while, when you came on the scene, he softened. But after you went away he went right back to being the same old Matt. I suppose that, seeing what he could be like, Rosemary saw no reason to go back to the old days.'

'She called him a pig as she left,' Carrie said vaguely, her mind trying unsuccessfully to sort out the facts.

'He's lucky she didn't say more,' Sylvia commented briskly. 'She thought a great deal more, I can tell you. What are you going to do?' she added quietly.

'Nothing. There's nothing that I can do. I even feel a traitor now, telling you all this.'

'We all need somebody to bounce ideas off,' Sylvia assured her.

'I haven't an idea in my head,' Carrie confessed.

'Things just seem to be swamping me. I'll be glad when we're back at Falconridge, at least there we've got breathing space.'

'Call me if you need me,' Sylvia reminded her as they parted later and Carrie nodded her thanks but she couldn't tell anyone really. She had told Sylvia about the ugly remarks that Lady Welland had aimed at her, but she had told her nothing else. The trouble lay too deep and was too private to share with anyone. It was ironic that the only person she would ever have told about such intimate matters would have been Matt and only Matt.

She stopped the taxi at the other side of the park, letting the twins run through the grass and enjoy the April sunshine before coming out through the little black wrought-iron gate to walk slowly and unwillingly to the flat.

She saw the Mercedes come roaring up from the underground garage as she was about a hundred yards away and watched it swing towards her, accelerating all the way.

Matt saw her as he tore past and the brakes were jammed on full as he stopped and spun round in the road, driving back past her to stop a few yards ahead. He was out of the car and on the pavement before they reached him and Carrie kept a tight grip on the two little hands in hers when the twins would have rushed to him.

'Where have you been?' he ground out before she had even reached him.

'Out.' She couldn't bear this feeling of being trapped, hated and despised.

'Where are you going now?' he rapped out, ignoring the twins, his eyes only for Carrie.

'To the flat! Where else?' she said with quiet bitterness. He watched her for a moment and she stood perfectly still, meeting his eyes, making her face as blank as possible, trying to contain the love that flooded through her even when he towered over her in anger.

'Get in. I'll take you back.' He opened the door but she ignored it, holding the twins back and meeting his eyes coldly.

'Thank you, we'll walk. We've been cooped up quite enough. Now we'll have freedom.'

She walked past him and when she came to the main doors of the luxurious block, taking her keys out of her bag, she glanced back. He was still there, staring after her, his face stony, but he did not come back himself and when she went to bed at ten o'clock, he was still out.

Over the next couple of days she hardly saw him at all. He merely came into the flat to change clothes and speak a little to Gemma and Pippa before leaving without a word to her and it was with relief that she answered the phone on Friday morning to hear John Carmichael's voice telling her that Falconridge was ready. Apparently, John was to drive her down there and a van would follow later with the toys and anything that could not go into the car. Ruby had already been taken back to Falconridge it seemed, but Matt was not going. He would be too busy in London.

Well, she had almost expected it. Apart from the fact that he had stayed at home since their marriage and would have to get back to work, it was very clear that he did not want to see her at all and was even prepared to forgo the pleasure of seeing the girls in order to avoid her. Allan, she knew, was now going into the main office to work with Matt there. They had clearly reached some sort of amiable under-standing although even Allan had told her nothing. Vivienne seemed to have been detailed to work with Allan and she knew that they were often out together in the evenings.

Allan seemed to have taken Matt's advice on the day of the wedding to heart. He was leaving her and

the twins to adjust to a new life. If he realised what a
miserable life it was, she knew he would be back to
fighting words with Matt, and as his future depended
on Matt she would never tell Allan of her latest
miseries.

Ruby didn't exactly put herself out to make John
Carmichael feel at home. She smothered the twins
with kisses, hugged Carrie as if she had just returned
from darkest Africa and looked in her severe way at
John before fetching him some coffee in a rather
grudging manner. It became very obvious why when
John had left and Ruby came to the point in her
direct way.

'I see you had to be brought home by strangers!'
she observed tartly. 'Where's Mr Matthew, then?'

'He's very busy, Ruby, and John Carmichael is no
stranger as you know very well. He's stayed here often
enough with his wife.'

'He's all right, I suppose,' Ruby conceded unwillingly, 'but it should have been your husband who
brought you home. He wasn't too busy to bring me
and to get all these men working on the grounds. He's
spent more time here than in London with you these
last two days, fussing over this and that. Piano's been
tuned,' she remarked finally and obscurely, walking
off to get lunch.

What the significance of that was, Carrie didn't
know. One thing was sure, the people who had done
the house had done it well. There was no sign that a
little while ago everything had been covered in a thin
layer of mud. The grounds, too, were getting a great
deal of attention because although there was now a
definite air of desolation about the parkland and the
gardens, there seemed to be about twenty men at work
out there. Even now their efforts could be clearly seen
to be winning over the battle with the river's destruc-
tive onslaught.

The river itself had now withdrawn, leaving small

unreal little lakes and pools that glittered unexpectedly from places where there had once been parkland. Carrie knew that this year, after all, there would be few daffodils. It seemed that, like her, Falconridge had taken a battering and was struggling to recover and appear normal. Its chances were better than hers, though, because no amount of effort and time was going to put the love that had once warmed this house back into Matt's heart.

He came later in the afternoon and his appearance took Carrie completely by surprise. Now that they were safely back at Falconridge she hadn't really expected to see much of him, and certainly not today. She caught sight of the Mercedes coming slowly round the circle of gravelled path that bordered the house. Matt stood for a while looking out towards the river before going to talk to the workmen.

His unexpected arrival panicked her. She felt suddenly shy and scared, not knowing whether to race off to her room and stay there until coming out became an absolute necessity or to face him straight away. In any case, whatever she decided to do would be of little importance, it was Matt who set the pace, Matt who made life either worth living or utterly impossible. She stood her ground and was in the drawing-room looking as unconcerned as she could manage when he walked in.

'Things have been done well, don't you think?' he said with no expression in his voice. 'Have you looked round?'

'Yes. There's no sign of damage anywhere in the house. There's only the grounds now. I expect they'll take a long time but they'll be back to normal by the time the flowers are out.'

Speaking to Matt like a stranger was not easy and he seemed to be having the same difficulty, his hands in his pockets, an air of restlessness about him that reminded her of how he used to be sometimes when she was still at Redland and he was outside waiting for her lectures to finish. Only then, he had relaxed as soon as he saw her. He wasn't going to relax now.

'Carrie,' he took a half-step towards her and what he had been about to say she never found out because the twins rushed in, delighted to see him, delighted to be back at the place they now called home. Carrie watched with an uneasy happiness as his face lit up at the sight of them and he crouched down to pull them both tightly to him, to listen to their chatter and talk to them, his face softening to real tenderness.

She knew that there was a wistful hunger on her face too and as Matt looked across at her, she turned abruptly and walked out. She was already too vulnerable. She couldn't afford to let him see how much she, too, needed his tenderness. She could still feel the lash of his words as he had left her after he had made love to her at the flat and she had already shed far too many tears. She was thankful that he loved the children and she would have to be content with that. He would be going back to town as soon as he could, she knew, probably to stay in the flat where he could telephone Florida in complete privacy, where he would not have to see her and be constantly reminded of her desertion.

He had insisted so many times that she had been the one to leave him that she now almost felt that it was true, and she was sure that only the flood had delayed his return to Florida after the letter.

He didn't go back to London, though, he stayed at Falconridge immersing himself in the work of restoring the grounds, spending each day out with the men, while Gemma and Pippa, well wrapped up, danced beside him enjoying the fresh air and his company. In the afternoons and evenings he was in the girls' room as often as not, helping them to sort out their treasures, talking to them, making up for the time he had missed and for his gloom at the flat.

He treated Carrie as a stranger, politely, pleasantly, but with no real warmth so that she was taken completely by surprise when he said briskly one morning, 'Get your jacket. It's time you were back out in the open air and anyway, they're just about ready to replant the things that we've lost from the garden. You'd better come and tell them what's missing if you want it to look as it did before.'

She was still stunned when, half an hour later, the orders issued, everybody waiting in silence until she had decided where things should be, Matt led his little band towards the now tranquil river.

The broken bank had been rebuilt and it was hard to believe that this quiet stretch of water, happily gurgling along had caused so much chaos.

'Well, it's back to normal until it decides to behave badly again.'

'You think it will?' she asked, instantly falling silent, feeling that she had been tricked into behaving and speaking normally, into letting her guard down.

'Oh, it's done it several times before apparently, but only in freak conditions, heavy snow followed by unusually heavy spring rains. We'll get along with no trouble, I expect. It's making the same old sounds now,' he added quietly.

Carrie looked away quickly. It was making the same old sounds, sleepy, contented sounds that she had heard so often as she lay in Matt's arms so long ago. She turned abruptly to the house without a word and went to her room, staying there until she heard Gemma and Pippa come tearing up the stairs later. Then she stayed with them, reading to them, playing with them, cutting Matt right out of her mind until presently she heard his car drive away. He didn't return for dinner.

It was after midnight when she woke with a start, knowing that someone was in the room and sure that it must be Gemma, hungry as ever, but it was Matt. He was standing beside the bed, looking at her and even in the light from the open doorway she could see how drawn he looked, how gaunt.

'Is something wrong?' She was instantly alert but he didn't answer.

'Matt?' She reached out for the bedside lamp but Matt's hand covered the switch immediately.

'Leave it! I'm sorry if I startled you.' He simply walked out closing the door and Carrie sat up in bed, switching on the light, thinking frantically. Something was wrong, she knew that. Something had brought Matt into her room and she felt that he had been going to tell her something, or ask her something. Maybe he was ill and needed her but couldn't bring himself to ask.

She shot out of bed and ran across the room, going straight into Matt's room without knocking, almost expecting to see him collapsed on the floor.

He was unbuttoning his shirt, clearly getting ready to go to bed and she had never seen him look so ill. His face was pale and drawn, his eyes red-rimmed and at the sight of her standing anxiously in the doorway, he turned away, not looking at her.

'I'm sorry I woke you up,' he said in a flat voice. 'You can go back to bed, we'll talk tomorrow.'

'Are you all right, Matt?'

'I'm perfectly all right. Go back to bed.' She didn't move and he turned round, his eyes dark shadowed.

'Look, we'll talk tomorrow. You'll get another cold, there's not much warmth in that nightdress and the heating has gone down for the night.'

'I—I'm sorry,' she blushed, realising that the sheer nightdress was allowing her body to be outlined against the light. 'I didn't think. I'll get my dressing-gown and then if there's anything that . . . '

'Don't bother!' he ground out. 'Can't you leave me alone?' She felt like a child who had been severely reprimanded for doing very little wrong and her head fell as she turned away.

'All right!' He crossed the room and took her arm, pushing her almost roughly into a chair. 'Sit there!' He moved away, his back to her as he spoke again. 'The other day, near the flat, you said you wanted freedom. That's why I came in tonight, to tell you that you can have as much freedom as you like. You needn't worry about Allan,' he added as he heard her little gasp of shock. 'Oddly enough, I've really taken to him, he's interesting to work with and I'll continue with him as normal. So long as I can see Gemma and Pippa frequently, I'll not oppose—a divorce.'

For seconds she sat completely still as everything she had dreaded unfolded before her eyes. He'd realised his mistake and he wanted Yvette. He would support his children in luxury, give her an enormous allowance and go to Yvette, or bring her here to Falconridge.

She stood up, the effort not to sway dizzily making her movements stiff and unreal, her skin suddenly icy cold and she was almost at the door before Matt turned and saw her.

'Carrie!' It wasn't the sound she had expected to hear. She had expected anger, frustration, not the cry of pain that her name became on his lips. It stopped her but she never turned, her whole body stiffly held in her own defence.

'It's want you want, isn't it, your freedom? I bullied you into marriage, we spend almost all our time locked in combat, the other night I damned near raped you. I don't suppose it was really a surprise to hear you talk about freedom.'

She never answered, never turned and after a few seconds of silence he continued, 'You seem to spend a lot of time hurt and unhappy. It's never been my intention to make you unhappy. The sooner we get this thing over, the better.'

'All right, Matt,' she managed in a tight little voice. 'If you want a divorce . . . '

'Me!' He strode to the open door, closing it, leaning

back against it. 'Why the hell should I want a divorce? I wanted you back!' His face tightened. 'Well, you're here, we're married and you kept your side of the bargain, but I can't keep mine.' He looked away, his face pale and drawn. 'I can't let you go on living in the past, looking over your shoulder, because I want you too damned much. I want you back in this room, back in my arms. I want the ghost out of your heart and the wistful look off your face. I've kept away just like I did when I first met you and I'm getting the same results. When you're finally gone, I'll have to face it, won't I?'

She couldn't really believe what he was saying. Yvette was as close, as real in her mind now as she had been over four years ago and the malicious voice of Cynthia Welland seemed to ring in her head . . . 'The only happiness he's ever had . . .'

'It doesn't matter . . . if there's somebody else . . . if you want . . .'

'I want you!' he said thickly, his eyes skimming over, bright with desire even in his distress. 'What do you want me to do—beg? Shall I get down on my knees? Shall I be pitiful and forlorn like Gemma? Is that what you want, the ultimate satisfaction of seeing me plead?'

She stood there hardly aware that she was staring at him with wide eyed amazement, her head shaking slowly from side to side. She didn't want him to beg, she only wanted him to love her with a mere fraction of the love she had for him and he reached out slowly, pulling her against him as he leaned against the door, looking down into her pale face, his eyes tortured his voice only just controlled.

'Carrie! I'm hungry—please!'

'Matt! Don't, oh, don't!' She stroked his face with anxious fingers, wanting to see him happy no matter what it cost and he caught her hand, raising it to his lips, his voice husky.

'I don't want a sacrifice, Carrie. Only if you want me, only if the nightmare can be over, only if you've come home.'

Every last bit of resistance left her in a great rush of love at the aching sound of his voice and her arms closed around him tightly, her fingers in his dark hair, her lips against his face.

'Matt! Oh, Matt!' was all she could say but it was enough for him and the kisses that now overwhelmed her were tender, gentle and filled with longing as he drew her close, seeking the past with an eagerness to match her own.

Nothing mattered except the feel of his arms, the feel of his body pressed close to hers. There was no one in the universe except Matt and herself as he swept her into his arms carrying her to the bed, and the joy as he possessed her was a mixture of the present and the past, the drift back to earth like the healing brush of wings, her name on his lips the sound of a lost melody.

'Don't move,' he murmured when at last she stirred beneath him. 'Let me go on feeling that you're part of me, that nothing has happened since the last time I held you like this in this room.'

Her languorous arms lifted to hold him, her hands to stroke the smooth power of his shoulders and he raised his head to look down at her, his eyes filled with a kind of wonder.

'You make me whole,' he said softly, his fingers threading through her hair. 'You feed my soul, give me a reason for being alive. You're a miracle I found and lost. Don't be lost again, Carrie.'

Even though the beautiful, delicate face of Yvette slid like a phantom through her mind, she clung to him fiercely, determined to live for now, for each day, determined to bury the past until it rose up again to strike her.

Her clinging arms, her desperate longing had him

looking at her with softly smiling eyes.

'Whatever it is that's troubling you, Carrie, it can't be real. This is real, you and I. Let the past go. Remember how we were, how we can be again. Just come to me.'

It was all she had ever wanted to do, just to come to him. There was no end to her love, there never had been and she was unaware that tears sprang to her eyes, that she whispered his name like a small lonely prayer. She only knew that he clasped her to him, kissing her with growing desire until she left the edge of the world in his arms and then sank into a sleep that was the only peaceful rest she had had since the last time she had belonged to him like this at Falconridge.

It was morning when she stirred to find that Matt was up and out of the room and as usual, tiny waves of fear raced across the peace of her mind, but when she hastily washed and put on her dressing-gown, she looked up to find him standing in the doorway, watching her quietly.

'We're just about ready for breakfast,' he said softly, leaning against the doorframe.

'I'll—I'll get dressed and come down,' she said almost in a whisper, unable to stop looking at him and unable to prevent the soft waves of colour that washed across her face as his eyes wandered slowly over her.

'Come as you are,' he said quietly, meeting her eyes. 'We're eating in the kitchen this morning. We've thrown Ruby into confusion but it's cosy.'

She went downstairs with him and it seemed that he was making a great effort to be easy-going. She wondered if he regretted the words he had spoken last night and she bit her lip in anxiety, almost afraid to speak in case the dream turned out to be nothing more than that.

'Mummy used to cook our breakfast in Australia,'

Pippa was telling Ruby as they entered and in spite of
Matt's assertion that Ruby was confused, she looked
remarkably smug to Carrie, a smugness that deepened
when she saw them come in together and glanced at
Carrie's flushed face. 'She made bacon and eggs,'
Pippa finished wistfully.

'And sausages,' Gemma added firmly.

'Well, perhaps she wants to make breakfast today,
then, as you're all in here,' Ruby remarked, looking
enquiringly at Carrie. 'I can find plenty to do around
the house and the cleaning woman is just about due
here.'

They were all looking at her in silence and Carrie
found herself smiling as she tied an apron round her
waist and took over the breakfast, preparing bacon,
eggs and toast, and sausages as Matt sat the children
at the table with cups of tea and watched her with
gleaming eyes that followed her wherever she moved.

'Mummy and I are going away for about three
days,' he finally announced in a voice that allowed for
no dissension. 'Ruby is going to look after you.'

'Matt!' There was a little panic in Carrie's voice as
the reason for Ruby's smugness dawned on her. She
had never left the children before and in any case,
nothing was settled between herself and Matt. They
still had their own separate secrets.

'I'm glad you like the idea,' Matt said determinedly,
'because it's all arranged. I've been very busy on the
phone this morning and we leave immediately after
lunch.'

'But . . . '

'No buts,' he insisted, 'it's all settled.'

'Where are you going?' the ever-inquisitive Pippa
wanted to know.

'I'm going to give Mummy a present,' Matt said
mysteriously and Gemma hugged herself with silent
pleasure.

'Is it good?' she wanted to know and Matt looked

at her eager eyes, her unselfish delight with a smile that was slow and warm.

'It's very good, my little mouse,' he assured her, 'but it's too big to wrap up and bring home.'

That stopped them completely and Matt's eyes met Carrie's in a shared smile as the twins silently puzzled over the likely things that were enormous.

'You are both going to have a good time because Uncle Allan and Auntie Vivienne are going to take you out each day.'

'Auntie Vivienne?' Carrie queried in surprise, dishing up the breakfast.

'I've been thinking about it and I've decided that it's coming along at a good pace,' Matt informed her. 'She battles on his side now and I reckon that when he goes back to Australia she'll be making the trip in some capacity or other. Do you mind?' he added, his eyes intently on her.

'No, of course not. I just want him to be happy and I think you're probably right. I think he needs someone who is—a character.'

'She's all of that!' Matt said with feeling. 'Anyway,' he added to the girls, 'they'll take you all over. There are lots of things to see in London.'

'Uncle Allan says there's a monster in the river some place,' Gemma said quickly.

'Uncle Allan is a . . . ' Matt began in annoyance but Carrie slipped in quickly.

'A good story-teller,' she finished warningly. 'There are no monsters in London,' she said with a finality that satisfied Gemma.

'Except for Uncle Allan,' Matt said under his breath, grinning as Carrie shot him a severe look.

When they finally left after an early lunch, Carrie had few misgivings. She trusted Ruby with the twins and Allan adored them. Matt had given no clues as to their destination but it didn't really matter where they were going, she only wanted to be with him wherever he went.

After last night, she had hardly known what to expect and Matt had surprised her. They both knew that nothing was really settled, that there were still great gaps to cross, gaps that desire would never fill, and Matt was a little strange today. His taut face had relaxed, he looked happier and more at peace, but there was still a tension in him that worried her and she could only think that he was battling the future out in his mind.

There was the great barrier between them of the years they had lost, and then there was Yvette. She had no idea what he had decided to do about that. Perhaps he had written to her or phoned her when he was alone in London or at Falconridge. If he went to Yvette, it would be so much more heartbreaking now. Last night she had allowed herself to slide into the past and she couldn't come back into a bleak world without him.

CHAPTER TEN

'WHERE are we going?' she asked as they sped north-wards and the London traffic cleared.

'Edinburgh,' Matt said calmly. 'I've bought you Princes Street. It's going to take some moving.'

She shot him a disgusted look and then said, 'Why buy a present, Matt? What for?'

'We got married,' he said quietly. 'It's a wedding present.'

'I didn't buy you one,' she exclaimed in sudden wide-eyed regret but he lifted her hand to his lips.

'You gave me Gemma and Pippa,' he assured her softly. 'I can't top that, I'm afraid.'

The warmth of the car and her contentment after so much strain finally closed Carrie's eyes and she only vaguely felt Matt let her seat back a little as she slid into sleep. They were climbing slowly in the thin sunshine of the late afternoon when she finally awoke and sat upright.

'We're in Yorkshire!' she said with certainty. 'We're in the Dales!'

'Ah! The old homing instinct,' Matt said knowledge-ably. 'The animal seeking its lair.'

'It's Hetherage!' she exclaimed, getting her bearings but Matt only smiled as he drove on through the village, never speaking until a few miles further on he pulled into the side of the road by a little white gate, a gate with a newly painted sign. Hawthorn Cottage.

She was still staring at the well-loved little house when Matt came round and opened her door, took her arm and led her through the gate and up the crazy-paved path to the house.

'Matt! Somebody lives here!' she whispered in embarrassment but he took a key from his pocket and dangled it in front of her.

'Not any more, Carrie. It's yours.'

She trailed behind him, unbelieving and he opened the door and motioned her inside.

'Truly,' he assured her. 'It's yours, Carrie.'

'Oh, Matt!' She threw her arms around him in a frenzy of love and delight and he hugged her close.

'Well, it cost a small fortune to persuade them to sell, but that makes it a bargain,' he said softly.

He let her go and she began to wander around in a dazed, happy way as he watched her with a smile.

'I couldn't find all the pieces of furniture that had been sold,' he said regretfully, 'but there's quite a few of your grandmother's things back here now. The woman in the cottage down the road has been a great help, she seems to have noticed where everything went.'

'Miss Danvers,' Carrie nodded. 'She was a friend of Grandma Ellie, she used to be the schoolteacher in Hetherage.' She stood still and looked at him quietly. 'Why did you do this lovely thing, Matt?'

He turned away, his hands in his pockets, his face out of her sight. 'Maybe I love you,' he said quietly.

There was a stillness about him that held her silent for a moment and she suddenly realised that he was afraid. Matt Silver was afraid in case she rejected him. He couldn't even look at her.

'I love you, Matt. I love you more than anything in the world.' He spun round as she spoke, looking at her with every part of him taut and then he strode across the few separating feet to pull her into his arms, rocking her against him silently, unable to speak.

After a few minutes, when she thought he would talk about almost anything else, he said rather shakily, 'I've had central heating put in. I hope you don't mind. It's well hidden but to me a coal fire is a thing to enjoy not to rely on. Grandma Ellie must have been an Amazon.'

'I expect it was her Viking ancestry,' Carrie said, shaking on her own account.

'Come in here,' Matt said huskily. 'I switched it on secretly as we came in. We'll be warm soon. We've got to talk.'

He kept his arm around her and they went into the little sitting-room she remembered so well and her eyes filled with tears as she saw the effort Matt had made to restore things to an order that she would recognise. She roamed around, touching the well-loved pieces, turning to Matt after a while with love and gratitude.

'When did you do this?' she asked tremulously.

'About two years ago,' he confessed, his eyes on her face. 'I—I needed to have something around me that— —that . . . Oh, God, Carrie, come here!' he cried in an agonised voice and when she ran to him, he sank into a chair, pulling her on to his lap.

'I spent a lot of time here,' he said huskily, 'talking to Miss Danvers, getting the place back to what it used to be like, sitting here thinking about you. Except it wasn't a comfort, really. It was like a museum until you came through that door.'

'I came up here when we first came back to England,' she said softly, nestling against him. 'I wanted to see it, to remember Grandma Ellie but all I succeeded in doing was thinking about you. I didn't know the cottage was empty.'

'You could have broken in and nobody would have minded,' he murmured, his lips brushing her forehead. 'I really was given the cold shoulder until I mentioned rather desperately that it was for you.'

'We were isolated and a bit clannish up here,' she said with a tremulous little laugh. 'I'm sorry you got the chilly treatment.'

'Ah, once I mentioned you I was really well in. The magic name Caroline Stuart had the whole village throwing open its doors. I stayed a lot at the Green Man at Hetherage. The landlord's a buddy of mine now.'

'He never told me about the cottage!' Carrie exclaimed indignantly, drawing back to look at him.

'When I knew you were no longer married,' Matt said, 'I phoned him to pass the word around that it was a secret, a wedding present.'

'Even before I said yes?'

'I had to have you back,' he said huskily, his arms tightening his lips stroking hers. 'I had to believe it would happen. It had to be real.'

She put her arms around his neck, her face against his, joyful about the love that had gone into this but fearful about the future.

'Oh, Matt,' she whispered. 'Don't leave me again. Don't go back to Yvette. I couldn't bear it. I couldn't!'

She felt his whole body stiffen and he pulled back to look at her, his face pale.

'You know about Yvette?' He seemed hardly able to get the words out and her heart sank as misery crept back into her mind.

'Yes.' It was only a whisper. 'I knew you went to her. You went so quickly and I thought you'd never come back. I thought . . . '

'I had to go,' he said slowly. 'She wanted me to go back.'

Icy cold waves rushed over her and she struggled to get up, to get away but he held her tightly.

'Let me go! Let me go!' It seemed to her that only speed would outrun the sorrow but Matt held her implacably.

'No, my darling. I'll never let you go again,' he said fiercely. 'I wanted to tell you right from the first about Yvette, but you were so fresh, so innocent that I didn't dare because I thought that I'd lose you and I couldn't face that. Well, I lost you anyway. Maybe if I'd been more open, more honest you would never have left me but everything must be out in the open now. You've got to hear about Yvette!'

She stopped fighting, sat still and tried to stifle the panic that had flared so quickly. Matt watched her with serious eyes before he began, choosing his words with care as if he too were afraid.

'When I asked you to come and live with me, to be my love,' he began gently, 'I didn't want to. I didn't want to be involved with a woman who could get close to me ever again.' His eyes roamed over her stricken face. 'But I fell in love with you. I couldn't live without you any more. I suppose that from the moment I saw you I felt that some kind of tragedy was bound to happen. I seemed to have lived a lot of life and you were so young, so new, like a shy flower. I tried to put you out of my mind, but I couldn't. The day I brought you the flowers I was giving myself a test, telling myself that as soon as I saw you in the light of day I'd realise the sheer stupidity of it, the madness, but when I saw you again, I just wanted to go right on seeing you. If you had refused the birthday dinner then I imagine that I would have been back again with some other excuse.

'I kept on trying, though. I tried to keep you at arm's length, terrified every day that you'd find someone of your own age and ask yourself why you were spending so much time with someone like me, lying awake at nights, longing for you. In the end I couldn't go on and when you came to me, it was like a miracle. You really seemed to love me deeply, not just some youthful infatuation and I was so deeply in love with you that I hardly dared to breathe. I should have asked you then to marry me, but I'd been in love before with Yvette and she had shown me how empty and foolish love was. I was too scared to see the difference. Blinded by the way I felt about you.'

She had stiffened as he had told her that he had once loved Yvette and he cupped her pale face in his hands, trying to put some warmth into her.

'Oh, Carrie, my love, don't grieve. Listen to me, then maybe you'll understand. Will you at least listen?'

She nodded and he drew her close, speaking against her hair, his voice soft and deep, his thoughts in the past.

'When I left Cambridge I was full of bright ideas, like Allan was when he launched his struggling little firm. There were two of us, Tim Davis and I, and we were filled with enthusiasm but little hard sense. We knew electronics, though, and America was the place, it was all happening there, so we went. We had no cash, only high-sounding qualifications and big ideas, but to our surprise, we succeeded. We got backing and we launched our firm.

'One of the backers was Yvette Carr, an actress, not films, stage. She didn't do big starring roles but she made a lot of money and she had a very shrewd business head. We began to expand, stretching the money to the limit but getting ready for the boom when it came. Well, it came but trouble hit us first—tragedy. We were in a car accident: Tim was killed and I had more bones broken than I knew I had.

'I was going to be a long time in hospital and like Allan, Tim and I had been doing the lot. Without us, everything ground to a halt and the backers wanted out. They came to tell me while I was in hospital but Yvette swayed them, she had a way with her, and after that she visited me often, at first to talk about the firm, later just to talk. I had no one to turn to and she somehow took over. By the time I was out of hospital the firm had been renamed Silver Electronics and Yvette was almost running it. I was grateful and I was utterly ensnared, she was intelligent, amusing and beautiful. I didn't know it then but she was also utterly ruthless. I was so besotted that I fell over myself in gratitude. I wanted to reward her and she got a good percentage of the shares. We planned to marry so it didn't really matter who had the shares to my mind.

'Then I discovered that I was not the only man in Yvette's life by any means, and she found the situation highly amusing. She also kept the shares. They were legally hers and there wasn't a damned thing I could do about it. I came back to London and built up this end of the business, gradually running down the American

end until all she could do was hang on to the shares
and argue. Quarrelling across the Atlantic by phone
proved to be a little costly and gradually she dropped
out of my life altogether. Every time she tried to use
her shares to influence anything, I beat her. I grew
ruthless myself and I swore that no other woman would
have even one tiny corner of my heart.' He tilted her
chin and looked into her eyes, his own golden eyes
smiling and warm.

'But then there was you, my sweet Carrie, and I fell
oceans deep without even knowing it was going to
happen. I realised that I felt for you a love that made
my feelings for Yvette seem shallow and childish, but I
was still too raw from that to put my life into your
hands, even though you put yours into mine. Yvette
wrote to me and told me that she had an incurable
blood disease and that she was dying. I trusted her not
one little bit but I found out that it was true. When she
sent for me, I felt that I had to go but I couldn't tell
you about her, even then.

'When I got there, she had already died and she had
landed everything in my lap. I had to deal with legacies
and a thousand and one things, her final laugh, I
suppose, but she willed the shares back to me so I
stayed and did everything she had wanted. But all *I*
wanted was you. I realised that I wanted to commit
myself to you for ever, I wanted to marry you, to be
able to look round and see you there for the rest of my
life and I was so happy, I hugged it to myself waiting
to walk back into Falconridge and pick you up and say,
"Marry me, my darling." When I came back, you had
gone and the whole nightmare seemed to be happening
again.'

'Oh, Matt!' Carrie's tears of pity fell like little pearls
and he kissed each one away. 'I thought that *you'd* left
me. I found the letter and the photograph when I was
tidying the drawers and she was so beautiful and you'd
gone so quickly that I thought you'd never come back.

She seemed to be everything that I'm not. I thought you loved her.'

'I never loved her. I realised that when I had you. I was too stupid to admit that I wanted to marry you so I lost you to someone else, to Haley!' he finished bitterly.

'I've always loved you,' she said softly, her arms around his neck. 'I've never loved anyone else but you. At first I was scared and shy but I knew that I wanted to be with you even if Allan disowned me and everyone else laughed at me. I've never loved anyone else but you.'

'Except Haley,' he said quietly, his face pale, his eyes hurt and pain-filled.

She felt an enormous weight of guilt that she had never told him the truth, found it impossible to excuse herself now that she understood, but it had to be said.

'There never was a Kevin Haley, Matt,' she told him anxiously, her eyes on his face as for a brief second he failed to take in this piece of unexpected information. 'We—we invented him, Allan and I . . . '

'But the ring, all you've said, the way you missed him, loved him . . . ' He just couldn't seem to realise that she had never loved anyone but him, it was too much to absorb, too much what he wanted to hear and he seemed unwilling to believe it.

'We picked a name at random,' she told him tremulously. 'Allan got the ring and I—I put it on myself. I was having Gemma and Pippa and I felt—felt . . . '

'Oh, Carrie! Oh, my darling!' Understanding of everything seemed to come to him at once and his love engulfed her in a great tide of tenderness and regret. 'You must have suffered so much, pregnant and alone. You must have been frightened. I can't understand why you don't hate me.'

'I love you, Matt,' she said softly. 'I was frightened, but more than that, I was lost without you and in the end, the twins were all I had of you. I never thought that I'd see you again. I couldn't seem to get over it even after four years.'

'Neither could I,' he whispered huskily, cradling her in his arms. 'I never will. I never felt in my life as I feel about you and it's going to last for the rest of our lives. I was angry and hurt and I began to look for you, telling myself that I would have revenge but knowing that I just wanted to have you back close to me. When I knew you were married, I nearly went mad, I thought that you were out of my reach for ever but I still had to bring you back to England, I still had to see you. When I saw you at that damned dinner, looking so lovely, I wanted to destroy everyone in the room.'

'Including me,' Carrie reminded him with a little laugh, her face still clouded at the memory.

'No,' he assured her softly. 'I just loved you. It was Haley I hated. I hated him with such ferocity that I could have torn him apart. But when I knew he no longer existed, I was determined to get you back. I was prepared to live with the knowledge that you still loved him and to hope that one day you'd forget.'

'I never told you about the girls,' Carrie said regretfully.

'Ah, the girls!' He suddenly smiled happily and kissed her deeply. 'When I saw the girls I had my first burst of hope. They were mine. I had not one little doubt about that. It gave me my first feeling of warmth inside to know that you'd had my children. I argued it all out in my head. You need never have gone through with it, but you did. You wanted them. I hung on to that very tightly.'

'I thought that you might not want them,' she said softly. 'When I found out that I was pregnant I thought that if I ever saw you again, if some miracle happened, you wouldn't want to be hampered with children.'

'Hampered!' He held her away from him and stared at her hard, making the colour rush into her face. 'Little idiot,' he said quietly, pulling her back against him. 'The first night at my flat, the first time that you belonged to me, I never thought about precautions. It happened so naturally, so beautifully, and I never gave a thought to the fact that someone so innocent and young wouldn't think about things like that. Then when you never mentioned it and nothing happened I thought that maybe you had taken precautions after all. You weren't a child and you'd been living in the city long enough to have talked to all the other students. Even then, I don't suppose it really dawned on me just how innocent you really were, what a miracle I'd found and possessed.'

He suddenly lifted her head and looked into her eyes, smiling ruefully. 'I'm not sorry,' he confessed. 'Every man wants the woman he loves to have his children, and they're so beautiful, such a joy. I could hug the three of you in my arms and never move for the rest of my life.'

'You said I could have a divorce,' she reminded him, smiling into his eyes.

'A momentary madness,' he growled, pulling her close. 'I was beginning to doubt my ability to keep my hands off you any longer and after that night, the night I was so savage to you, I knew I had to do something drastic. I couldn't wait for things to happen. I had to make them happen. There was no way that I was going to stop coming for more. Only I thought that your unhappiness was because you loved Haley still.'

'I should have told you straight away,' Carrie sighed regretfully, 'but I was jealous of Yvette and frightened that you'd go back to her.'

'And I was jealous of Haley, jealous that you'd belonged to somebody else, jealous of a figment of your imagination. I realised that I'd never been in love in my life until I met you. The women that I'd known were momentary interests. When I saw you, for a few seconds I think I totally stopped breathing. It was a really terrifying feeling. I stood talking to you, thinking to myself, "So this is what it's like, this is being in love." You made me feel really humble.'

'Humble!' She stared at him, laughing. 'You were terribly autocratic.'

'A good act, I thought,' he laughed, turning her face up to his. And then the laughter died on both their faces as they looked deeply into each other's eyes.

'Carrie,' he whispered, his lips finding hers in a deep aching kiss that she needed so badly and her arms wound around his neck, her lips opening beneath his with the old remembered sweetness.

'We can have dinner at the Green Man,' he said unevenly after a while, but she shook her head.

'I don't want to move away from you. We can eat here if there's any food in the cottage.'

'A well-stocked refrigerator,' he murmured huskily. 'We can have a midnight feast—afterwards.'

She opened her eyes and saw the desire blazing in his as he looked down at her.

'It's been a long time since I had you all to myself,' he said thickly, his hands moving impatiently over her. 'We've got four years to make up for, four years of wanting you.' His lips closed over hers as she clung to him. 'I want you now,' he breathed desperately.

Later, as they lay in each other's arms, Matt staring thoughtfully at the ceiling, he said quietly, 'I'm thirty-seven, nearly thirty-eight.'

'You poor old thing!' She leaned over him, teasing his lips with hers and suddenly found herself beneath him again as he looked down at her with laughing eyes.

'I said that, not so much to incite pity as to impart information,' he said severely, his hands beginning to excite her all over again. 'In my opinion, it's time we had another baby, or do you intend to go on producing matching sets?'

'My mother and Allan's were identical twins,' she informed him, softly reminiscent. 'I expect that's why Allan and I are so close.'

'I don't know if that assertion has any basis in fact,'

he laughed, looking at her with adoring eyes, 'but I'll have it investigated. I'm really willing to believe anything you tell me though, my love, and if you want to have children in twos, then I honestly don't mind a bit.'

'You're wanting another wedding present,' she teased.

'Oh, about that, there is something you can do for me,' he murmured, moving to the side and taking her with him, his arms enfolding her closely. 'I want you to get Rosemary back for me. I have her address and she's not working at the moment and I thought that if you were to go and . . .'

'Matt Silver! You cunning man! Why don't you go yourself?'

'She'd slam the door in my face and if I put my foot there, she'd crush it,' he said with certainty. 'She packs a lot of weight.'

'All right. But I can't keep promising to give you people as presents,' she warned him. 'I'll take the twins and try to talk her round. What about Barton?'

'I thought that I'd promote her,' he grinned craftily. 'Somewhere where things are a bit slack. She knows how to put fire into the troops. Now that you're back, I can't manage her and when I stay at home just to make love to you, she'll reprimand me, get out of hand. I'm too soft when you're around to cope with Barton. You're giggling again,' he added softly. 'Does that mean that you're happy?'

'You know I am,' she whispered, trailing her fingers through his hair, her eyes filled with wonder. 'I can't believe that it's true, that I'm back with you again, that you love me.'

'I told you,' he said deeply. 'I loved you the moment I saw you. I came across that room to get you out of there with all possible speed and into bed as quickly as I could,' he added, grinning as her face flushed deeply. 'But when you turned and looked at me with those big, beautiful, violet eyes, I'd lost the battle before it had even begun. I just wanted to love and protect you for ever.'

'The violets at the church surprised me,' she confessed. 'I didn't know what to think when I got to the church and there was that lovely bouquet.'

'You imagined that I'd let my love go into a cold church with no music, no flowers, no bouquet?' he asked. 'I couldn't wipe out the four years at one go but I wanted you to feel that it was a real marriage, as beautiful as I could make it under the circumstances.'

'Even before you know that Gemma and Pippa were yours?' she asked in wonder.

'It was you I wanted, not the children,' he whispered softly, his hands stroking her skin, his lips against her face. 'I've never wanted anyone but you since the moment I saw you, I never will. The girls are part of us, part of our love, but you are my darling. When you agreed to marry me, I knew I would have to go very carefully but I was willing to do anything to get you back completely, even though I thought you'd just simply walked out and left me. I love you too much to manage without you.'

'I told myself that I was doing it for Allan's sake, but deep down I knew that I just wanted to be near you,' she sighed, 'and when you called me Carrie at that little hotel, I was so happy even though I knew it was a mistake.'

'I don't do things by mistake,' he asserted fiercely. 'I had to go carefully, that's all. If I'd known that the wistful looks were for me and not for Haley, we should have been here weeks ago, all by ourselves.'

'You had a letter from America at the flat,' Carrie reminded him softly, wanting to clear everything out of her mind except the love she felt for the man who held her close.

'And you thought it was from Yvette?' he sighed deeply and kissed her. 'Oh, Carrie, if only I'd known, we could have saved you so much more misery. It was from Yvette's brother, just a little letter of thanks because now everything has been sorted out properly. He invited both of us to visit him whenever we wanted.'

'He knows about me?'

'I think that perhaps I've become a bore,' he grinned.
'I tell everyone who'll listen. The night we got so wet at
Falconridge, I even told Allan.'

'So that's why you two suddenly became friendly!
What did you tell him?' she demanded to know.

'That I love you, that I've loved you since I saw you
and I'll never let you go.' His voice was like music from
the past, deep, warm and loving, his eyes worshipping
her as he pulled her close to the hard warmth of his
body. 'When you told me that night at Falconridge that
making love with me would be second best, it nearly
killed me,' he added soberly.

'Oh, Matt, darling, I didn't mean that! I thought you
just wanted me and I couldn't forget what it used to be
like. I wanted the beautiful memories with me for ever.
No matter how I wanted you, I couldn't let the memories go, I had to go on dreaming.'

'And I thought you were dreaming about Haley,' he
growled.

'There is not and never has been a Haley,' she
reminded him. 'Let it go, Matt.'

'I'll let everything and everyone go, except you,' he
assured her, moving over her. 'There seemed to be no
point in being alive while you were away. No wonder
Rosemary left. I was a pig, it's true.'

'That reminds me,' she insisted, her hands pressing
against the hard power of his chest, determined to get
the last word. 'Just what illness was I supposed to have
suffered from while I was away?'

'What?' He looked down at her, clearly amazed.

'You said that you would tell everyone that I had
been ill. Ruby clearly believes that I've been ill. So,
what did I suffer from? It's as well to know in case I
get it again.'

Her eyes were laughing into his and he grimaced
ruefully.

'An empty threat,' he confessed. 'I didn't tell anyone
anything. You and I are secret, haven't we always been

secret? We never let anyone really close to use. You imagine that I would go round telling people about our private affairs? You've always been my private affair,' he added teasingly.

'Well, Ruby thinks that I've been ill,' she insisted, turning her head to avoid his lips. 'She said I hadn't known what I was doing because I was so ill.'

'Ruby,' he said firmly, 'is an incurable romantic. She couldn't face the possibility of our separation, so she made up her own reasons and stuck to them. Many times while you were away from me I've been close to giving her the sack for talking about you and how you wandered off so ill, how I'd better find you. God! It's all I ever wanted to do with the rest of my life, but she kept on pushing the medicine right down my throat. Anyway,' he added, 'you didn't know what you were doing, did you? You just wandered off, lonely and lost.' He pulled her face round to his, almost rough in his desire. 'Stop talking, stop tormenting me, I love you! I want you!'

She sank into the drowning waves of his passion, home at last, safe from the world, listening to the sound of her own name on his lips as if there had been no time in between. It didn't matter where they were as long as they were together. Wherever Matt was, there was home, there was all the love she would ever need.

FINDING LOVE TWICE IN A LIFETIME.

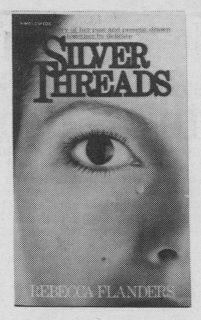

Scientific research and foreign agents force a girl to assume a new identity. Her past is all but wiped out.

At a chance meeting in a skiing chalet, Amanda finds herself strangely attracted to Craig. He in turn is reminded of a woman he once loved.

Amanda's Victorian seafront house in Seattle, and the memories of a Florida beach finally provide the missing pieces to a puzzling jigsaw of love and intrigue.

A powerful new novel from Rebecca Flanders.

Price: £2.25 Available: July 1987 **W●RLDWIDE**

Available from Boots, Martins, John Menzies, W. H. Smith, Woolworths, and other paperback stockists.

 **ROMANCE**

Next month's romances from Mills & Boon

Each month, you can choose from a world of variety in romance with Mills & Boon. These are the new titles to look out for next month.

STRIKE AT THE HEART Emma Darcy
THE CHAUVINIST Vanessa Grant
HONEYMOON ISLAND Marjorie Lewty
TAGGART'S WOMAN Carole Mortimer
HEART OF GLASS Dana James
OPEN TO INFLUENCE Frances Roding
TIME OUT OF MIND Kay Thorpe
NIGHT TRAIN Anne Weale
PASSIONATE REVENGE Sally Wentworth
THIS MAN'S MAGIC Stephanie Wyatt
*__TEMPORARY PARAGON__ Emma Goldrick
*__AUTUMN AT AUBREY'S__ Miriam MacGregor
*__BRING BACK YESTERDAY__ Rachel Ford
*__BITTER INHERITANCE__ Kate Kingston

Buy them from your usual paperback stockist, or write to: Mills & Boon Reader Service, P.O. Box 236, Thornton Rd, Croydon, Surrey CR9 3RU, England. Readers in Southern Africa — write to: Independent Book Services Pty, Postbag X3010, Randburg, 2125, S. Africa.

*These four titles are available from Mills & Boon Reader Service.

Mills & Boon
the rose of romance